TM

Superman Returns
The Last Son of Krypton

by Brandon T. Snider

Superman created by Jerry Siegel and Joe Shuster

First edition. Printed in USA.
All rights reserved.
ISBN: 0-696-22959-5

We welcome your comments and suggestions.
Write to us at: Meredith Books, Children's Books,
1716 Locust St., Des Moines, IA 50309-3023.

meredithbooks.com

Table of Contents

PROLOGUE
The Last Son
of Krypton

Superman. The Man of Steel.

He has the strength to move mountains. His breath is like a snowstorm. He can fly high into the sky. But Superman often dreamed of his home planet, Krypton, and when he went looking for it, he wasn't prepared for what he found.

This is where the story begins.

1
Warworld

He awoke in an unfamiliar place, having no idea how or when he got there. His mind was confused, his memories hazy. He believed he was in space looking for something he couldn't find. Now he was in a dirty prison cell on an unfamiliar planet, surrounded by the filth of the galaxy.

I'm not a criminal, so what am I doing here? Superman thought.

Looking around, he noticed the others in the cell: aliens, monsters, criminals from all over the universe, all of them fighters. He felt their harsh stares. Their hands gripped the iron bars that caged them, their arms reached to tear the clothing from his back. Every single one of them knew who he was, what he stood for, and where he came from. All of them wanted to take him down. But today they would have to wait. Today he belonged to someone else.

"Get up, whelp! Did you enjoy your sleep?" the guard asked as he struck Superman in the face with his staff. A thin line of blood ran down Superman's cheek as he slowly rose to his feet.

"It's time to fight, and Mongul will not be kept waiting!" the guard barked.

Superman staggered a bit, his senses blurred by the blow and by the unbearable prison conditions. He straightened up and spoke to the guard.

"Do not call me whelp," he ordered as if he were the one in charge.

"Ha! You're a mouthy one, aren't you? Get moving!"

He was the greatest super hero the world had ever seen. But not this

world. Far away from anything or anyone he had ever known, this once-great hero was now reduced to a mere prisoner. And his captors couldn't have been happier.

"Where am I?" he asked.

"You're on Warworld," the guard explained, yanking Superman by his chains and dragging him down a darkened corridor.

"How did I get here?" he pressed on.

"Do you not recall your journey? Your pretty Kryptonian ship floated into our atmosphere. Mongul recognized its origin and took it. Little did he know that the last son of that destroyed planet was inside, wrapped in his mother's precious blanket! Ha! Ha! Ha!" the guard cackled.

Superman, the Man of Steel, stayed on his feet despite his exhaustion. His once-clean Kryptonian garb was now covered in dirt and sweat. Confused, Superman appealed again to the guard. "What goes on here? Where are you taking me?"

"The beatings at the hands of our best warriors must have caused you to lose your memory, eh? This is Warworld, a planet of pure destruction. A planet that separates the weak from the strong through combat. Here, only the strongest survive, and the weak are destroyed. For the past 10 days, you've battled and beaten the most powerful men on Warworld, if not the entire galaxy. Do you not remember this? Well, no matter. Mongul will end all of it today."

The Man of Steel grew angry.

"Who is Mongul?" Superman demanded.

The guard roared with laughter, then composed himself and addressed Superman's question.

"Mongul is your leader, whelp! He is the ruler of Warworld, and you'd do well to remember that when he is destroying you!"

The guard struck him across the face with his staff yet again. Superman touched his skin and felt a fresh trickle of blood, an unfamiliar feeling for a man whose skin had always been impervious. Superman's mind began to race as he recalled his most recent adventures.

This can't be right. I was in space. I was looking for the remains of my birth planet. Scientists had discovered that Krypton might still be out there, so I set off to look for it. I'd been traveling for months? Years?

I don't remember. When I arrived, I found a large chunk of rock that I thought was part of Krypton, but it was just kryptonite, the substance that makes me weak and steals my powers. Even though I was weak, I was able to make it back to my ship. I told the ship to return to Earth and then . . . then I can't remember . . . .

Superman quietly drifted in and out of consciousness as the guard dragged him through the darkened catacombs, depositing him before the stone door that opened to the coliseum. He collapsed.

"When this door opens, you will meet your fate at the hands of the master. Look at you. You're weak! It's a shame. What is the Earth phrase? 'Good luck' isn't it? HA! HA! HA! Good luck then, whelp!"

And with that, the guard kicked Superman squarely in the stomach, knocking every last ounce of air from his lungs. Gasping for breath, he tried to relax himself. He thought back to the days when he was a little boy on Earth. He thought of his mother in Kansas. How sweet would her strawberry pancakes be right about now? He thought of his friends at the *Daily Planet*. He thought of his pal, Jimmy Olsen, taking his picture, and he smiled. He thought of Lois Lane.

As the stone doors opened, a bright white light burned his exhausted eyes.

"Get up. It is time."

This might be the end, Superman thought.

2
Mongul

Mongul! Mongul! Mongul! Mongul!" the crowd in the coliseum roared. Their leader sat down on his throne, smiling at the attention, his deep-red eyes burning into Superman, and the amulet on his chest glowing with the energy of the sun. Mongul dreamed of challenging Superman, and now the Kryptonian had been delivered to him. He had invaded and conquered countless worlds, exploring the galaxy from the planet known as Warworld, making entire populations his slaves. Mongul found great pleasure in the suffering of others, and today he would find pure joy in the defeat of Superman. Rising from his throne, Mongul slowly walked down to the arena floor where he would do battle.

Throughout the entire galaxy, there was only one name that struck fear in the hearts of every creature that heard it: Mongul. His story was simple. He was a former leader of a planet and was banished from his home world. He swore he'd conquer his world again and take back his throne. To do this, he sought out the most powerful weapon in the universe: the planet Warworld. He conquered it easily and began gladiatorial games to amuse himself as well as the people over whom he ruled. The games quickly turned into a dangerous fight club as creatures from all over the galaxy challenged each other for the ultimate prize: control of Warworld. All they had to do was defeat Mongul.

At the other end of the arena, a broken and battered Superman was

pushed onto the floor. The giant stone doors shut behind him, trapping him inside with his captor. Superman's vision was hazy as he focused on the figure across the arena and saw the giant Mongul staring back at him, his arms and legs like stone, his chest plate glowing with a bright-yellow energy. The time had come again to fight, but for the first time in his life, Superman doubted himself. Would this be his end? Would he ever make it back to Earth? *No*, he thought, *there is no time for doubt*. There was only time for fighting.

Mongul made his way toward the middle of the arena and stopped. He nodded and offered his hand to the Man of Steel.

Superman shook his head, puzzled that someone so evil would attempt to show any kind of manners. Using every bit of strength he could, he stood up and approached Mongul. The crowd fell silent as the two powerful beings met.

Mongul grinned and leaned down to whisper into Superman's ear, his breath so hot that it almost burned his skin.

"Goodbye, Kryptonian."

Quicker than light, Mongul's enormous fist knocked Superman off his feet and sent him flying across the arena. The crowd roared in delight.

Before he could catch his breath, Superman saw his enemy charging at him like a rhinoceros. Seeing no way out, he attempted to fly up and over Mongul. He ran toward Mongul and jumped. However, because Superman was weak, his jump was not high enough. Mongul grabbed him by his leg and swung him around in a circle, making Superman dizzy. Mongul let go, and Superman went flying into the stone wall of the arena.

Mongul watched Superman recover from across the arena and wondered if the stories he'd heard were true. This "Superman" was supposed to be powerful, but today he appeared to be weak. Mongul slowly approached him, taking his time and enjoying the pain he had given his opponent.

"The people of Warworld demand a fight to the end. Won't you give it to them, Last Son of Krypton?"

Superman looked up and finally spoke to Mongul.

"I don't know what your problem is, Mongul, but I'm going to give

you one chance to end this."

"Oh, I will end it." And with that, Mongul once again punched Superman with his rock-hard fists. Superman tried his best to roll with each punch. But he was weak; he was no match for Mongul's power.

The crowd clapped and cheered as they watched the match. Out of breath and out of energy, Superman's eyes blurred as Mongul grabbed him and lifted him up to give him one last bit of advice.

"It looks as if you're in pain. Do you know pain, Kryptonian? I know pain. When I was young, I watched as my mother gave birth to another child. A boy. Having a brother would mean that I would be challenged for affection as well as power. So while my brother was sleeping, I destroyed his crib and him along with it. A small sacrifice I made in my search for ultimate power. And now there isn't anyone in the universe I won't destroy. I always hoped that Superman would provide me with the challenge I had so dreamed of. But look at you! You're hardly the man you once were. I will enjoy stealing your final breaths."

Suddenly, Superman noticed something. His muscles felt tighter, his joints were finally able to move without pain. His skin began to tingle a little. His powers returned to him. *But how could this be?* He knew his body was able to store energy from the sun. That was the source of his amazing powers. Unfortunately, in the darkness of space he had slowly been losing his powers—until now. The change must have had something to do with Mongul. Before he could form his next thought, Mongul slammed him into the ground.

"It is time for the end. Goodbye, Superman."

Mongul took a few steps back. He stopped for a moment. This was to be his greatest defeat ever, and he wanted to enjoy it. He closed his eyes, threw his head back, and took a deep breath. But as he opened his eyes again, he was shocked to see that his enemy had disappeared.

"What? What kind of joke is this?" he screamed.

"It is no joke at all, Mongul, just poor planning," said a voice from behind his back.

Mongul turned to see the Man of Steel standing and waiting behind him.

"How about a hug?" Superman asked, stone-faced.

Superman squeezed Mongul, using every ounce of his strength. But instead of weakening, Superman's power grew until he was finally at full strength. He squeezed tighter, then dropped the stunned and weakened Mongul onto the floor of the arena.

"Thanks for the power boost!" Superman said, grinning.

The breathless Mongul stared up at the Man of Steel and, in a desperate move, he raised his fists, ready to punch Superman into the ground. However, the newly energized Superman was one step ahead of him and threw his own punch, stopping Mongul for good.

"You know, Mongul, I couldn't figure it out at first, but then I realized that every time you got close to me, I started to feel better. I thought it was your magnetic personality, but then I realized that it was the yellow amulet on your chest. It's solar energy, isn't it? That just happens to be what I get my powers from. I guess we do have something in common. Thanks for your help!"

As the defeated Mongul lay before Superman, he quietly began to cry. Superman leaned down and offered his hand to Mongul.

"Thank you, Superman," Mongul said as he squeezed Superman's hand tightly, "but you and I have nothing in common."

Mongul yanked Superman by the hand and threw him against a stone column, causing it to collapse and cover the Man of Steel in rubble. The people of Warworld cheered as Mongul raised his fist in victory.

"Hey, Mongrel!" Superman called out. "How about a little batting practice?"

As he rose from the rubble, Superman grabbed one of the fallen stone columns and slammed Mongul across the arena.

"This ends now, Last Son of Krypton!!!" Mongul swore from 60 feet away. He grabbed another fallen column and charged Superman. The two men were engaged in a fierce battle. Again and again the two powerful men struck their blows until Superman noticed Mongul weakening and seized his chance for victory.

"Sorry, Mongul, but this is the end of the road," Superman announced as he raised his stone weapon and hit Mongul hard enough to drive him into the ground, ending the battle for good. He reached down and tore the amulet from Mongul's chest, leaving him shattered and powerless. Superman then ripped a steel beam off the stadium. Using

his heat vision, he melted the metal and tied it around Mongul, keeping him from escaping. He turned to the crowd and announced the defeat of their leader.

"People of Warworld, Mongul has been defeated! You will no longer have to live under his evil rule. It's time for you to . . ."

At that moment Superman noticed that the people had softly begun chanting. The chant kept building until it became a roar that filled the stadium.

"Kill Mongul!! Kill Mongul!!! Kill Mongul!!!!"

Superman paused. *Is that really what these people want?* he thought.

He looked out at the crowd: The people stared right back. It was clear—they wanted Mongul's death. They wanted destruction, because it was all they knew. The chant grew louder and more demanding. Superman took a moment to think, then let out an equally loud response.

"QUIET!!!!" His powerful voice rocked the stadium. The chant stopped. The gathered creatures stood mesmerized.

"Killing Mongul is not the answer. He should be punished for his crimes, but there will be no killing here today. You are free people now. You're free to make your own choices. But it's up to you to also make the right choices. You no longer need these contests to tell you who the strongest leader is. Each and every one of you is strong. It's up to you to rebuild this planet brick by brick. The days of Warworld are over!!"

A tired voice cried out as one of the spectators moved out of the crowd to address Superman.

"Superman! Please, you must help us! You do not understand. Mongul was everything. He took care of us. Without him, we are nothing. You must stay with us! Please!"

The Man of Steel paused. He wondered if the man was right. All these people knew was violence, and Mongul offered comfort in his own strange way. *Is that what they want? Someone who will tell them what to do? Someone to blindly follow?* He finally found the words and spoke to the crowd, his voice as warm as ever.

"It's up to you to take care of each other. Let the strong support the weak instead of destroying them. Let young and old, weak and strong alike, work together to start over. I can't stay here to help, but I will

return one day, and I expect to see a new world filled with hope."

The people of Warworld had never known such kindness and understanding. Though they knew it would take a long time to change, one by one the crowd slowly came to understand Superman's message, and cheers rang out across the stadium.

As he looked down at the defeated Mongul, Superman felt sorry for him. All he ever knew was terror and violence, so it's all he ever showed to others. Superman thought of his family on Earth, and it made him happy.

"Guard! I have defeated Mongul, so that makes me the new leader of Warworld, does it not?"

"Yes, Superman, it does," the guard quickly agreed as he began to kneel.

"Good. Then you'll do as I say," Superman said as he stood the man up. "You are to put Mongul in one of your cargo ships. Take him to the prison planet Takron-Galtos, where he will be locked up with around-the-clock security. And I'm to be informed of any and all changes in his condition. Do you understand?"

"Yes, sir!" the guard said, nodding in agreement.

"Good. Now, if you'll show me to my ship, I'll be on my way," Superman said, eager to get home.

The guards hurried to retrieve Superman's ship and returned with it a minute later. Damaged when it was captured, the Kryptonian ship had since repaired itself and was now completely restored. Superman turned to address the people one last time.

"Goodbye, citizens of Warworld. I will be watching," Superman called out as he climbed into the ship. Stopping for a moment and turning to face the crowd once more, he offered one last bit of comfort for the people of Warworld. "Have faith," he said.

And with that, the hatch closed. The crystal ship rose out of the dust and dirt and through the hatch opening in the arena ceiling, rocketing deep into space. It was time for Superman to settle in for a quiet journey. He said one simple word before he went to sleep. "Home," he whispered.

3
Nightmare!

"Superman! Superman, please help us!"

He heard the pleas from all over the city, but there was no time to think, only time to act. Superman had to make a difficult decision. As a deadly meteor shower rained down upon Earth, he had to make a choice.

"Superman, you've got to save me!" said Lois Lane from atop the Daily Planet Building, as a meteorite headed straight for her.

Superman wondered if he should save the woman he loved or the people he had promised to protect.

"Clark? Clark? Aren't you going to save me? You wouldn't forget about your mother, would you?"

Superman turned around and was shocked to see his mother standing in front of him.

"Ma? What are you doing here?" Superman asked, stunned. "You've got to find shelter. This isn't a safe place for you to be."

His worst nightmare had come true. Everything around him was crashing down, and the people that meant the most to him were caught right in the middle. He had nowhere to turn. He couldn't possibly save everyone at once, but what should he do? How could he make the choice to save one life and allow another to end?

"Kal-El, my son . . . the Last Son of Krypton . . . it is time for you to rise," said Jor-El. Superman was once again shaken at the sight of another of his loved ones. But this time, the pieces of the puzzle

came together, and he realized that all was not what it seemed. The appearance of his birth father, Jor-El of Krypton, confirmed it. The stress of his journey into space had at last caught up to him. His mind was playing tricks on him. He was dreaming.

"Father!" Superman cried. He awoke in a cold sweat, shaking. This wasn't an ordinary dream. It was a nightmare, the worst nightmare he had had since he left Earth. He felt around him to make sure everything was okay. He was safe inside his crystal spaceship. He wiped his brow and looked out among the stars. Soon he'd be home, but for now he was alone in the solitude of space.

A holographic image appeared before him.

"Kal-El. Son. When your mother, Lara, and I placed you in this ship and sent you to Earth to save you from Krypton's destruction, we created these crystals to help you adjust to your new home. We knew, because of the great powers you would develop, that things would not be easy for you. You would have to make choices, and not all of them would be simple."

Superman spoke to the image.

"But father, I left them. I left them to look for you. I don't know if I can return to Earth and continue being who I once was. With all the powers I have, I can only do so much. The people have to understand that I can't do everything. I'm not some sort of god. I'm just like them."

"Your feelings are logical, but you must realize that you're not like them."

"But I am!" Superman shouted back. "I am like them! These powers don't make me any different on the inside." Superman stopped. "The people think I'm so special because I have powers and I can fly, but that's not the only thing that makes me special. Like any human I am special because of who I am and should be valued for that alone. When I return to my life on Earth, I don't know if I'll ever be able to live up to their expectations. I don't think I can return to them as Superman."

"Your gifts are unique. It would be a terrible waste for you not to use your powers to help others," Jor-El's image said.

"But I can't do everything. How will people ever grow and change if I'm always there to save them? How will they ever learn to do anything for themselves?" Superman pushed on.

14

"You underestimate the people of Earth, son," Jor-El explained. "They are learning. They are wiser than you think. You must help them find the right direction. Guide them with your wisdom, and if they fall, you must be there to catch them."

As the image of his father faded, Superman shook his head. Thoughts of the future swirled in his mind. He was so close to home, but what would happen when he returned? Would the people welcome him, or would they turn against him? But those questions would be answered soon enough. He double-checked the ship's coordinates. They were indeed set for Earth. He breathed a sigh of relief, closed his eyes, and fell asleep.

4
Finally Home

Martha Kent had been up since 4:30 in the morning. Before most people started their day, she had finished half of hers. Life on the farm was all she knew and all she needed. When her husband, Jonathan, had passed away, life on the farm changed. Things got a little harder, and she got a little lonelier, but she always had her son to confide in. To her, Clark was a gift, and he was given powers so special that they were their little secret. A few years ago, Clark went away and Martha felt lost and alone. But today those feelings were gone. Today her son had returned. She had always had faith that he would. Never asking any questions and never wondering too much, she knew that no matter where her son was or what he was doing, he would return. That day was today, and Martha Kent couldn't have been happier.

"Clark? Clark Kent! Are you rustling around up there?" she asked, ready to give him the welcome-home hug she'd been holding for hours.

As Clark made his way to his mother, his senses became clearer. His body was no longer weakened by the darkness of space, but energized by the sun's rays. Looking out the front door of the farmhouse on the fields of golden wheat, he sighed. At last, he was home.

A panic suddenly gripped him as he sensed something overpowering him, causing him to lose control. He stopped, inhaled, and realized what it was. Strawberry pancakes.

"Are you going to stand there all day, or are you going to come in

and eat your breakfast?" Martha chided.

"Ma!" Clark cried. He had waited for this moment for years. He ran to his mother and embraced her, then picked her up and spun her around the room.

"I've missed you so much, Ma. There wasn't a day that I didn't think about you. I have so much to tell you."

"And I want to hear all about it, Clark. But right now, I need you to go move that ship of yours before the neighbors see it. Then you've got to get something in your stomach! You look like you haven't eaten in forever."

Clark went out to the field where the crystal ship had landed, and, using one hand, he lifted it up and gently flew it over to the barn where, in his childhood, he found it all those years ago. *Here's where my parents kept it, the ship they found me in. They waited to tell me about it until I was old enough to accept my destiny. But I still don't know what my destiny is*, Clark thought.

While in the barn, he noticed something sitting on a bale of hay. It was his mother's scrapbook. In it, she chronicled all of his adventures through the years. She must have left it in the barn by accident. He picked it up. Just as he was about to look through it, his mother called to him from the house.

"Clark! C'mon, son. The pancakes are getting cold!" Martha called from the porch.

Clark tucked the book under his arm and ran inside. Returning from the barn and his chore, he was finally able to enjoy breakfast.

"Go on, dig in!" Martha smiled. And he did; it was good.

"Sorry if I woke you up last night," Clark said, as he stuffed pancakes into his mouth.

"Well, it was a little unexpected. And I did have to make up a story to tell the neighbors. Can't exactly tell them a spaceship landed in my yard last night and that my boy is home from outer space. I told them some raccoons got into the trash. They'll never know the difference!" she giggled.

Hours passed as mother and son talked. Clark told his mother about everywhere he'd been and everything he'd seen.

"Oh, son, I'm so sorry you didn't find what you were looking for.

17

I know how much finding your home planet meant to you," Martha comforted.

"Ma, Earth is my home. I just wanted to know . . . more. I wanted to see if the reports were true, if Krypton really was still out there. I wanted to see what it was like, what the people were like . . . . " He stopped himself, noticed his mother's face, and realized how much he had left behind.

"Honey, you don't have to explain. I understand. But now, who is this Mongul character? He had you trapped in some sort of fighting club? That's just horrible."

As the two of them chatted about the past, his mother became more concerned with the future.

"What are you going to do now that you are home, Clark?" Martha asked.

"I figure I'll stay here for a while. Work on the farm. Have you heard from any of my old friends lately?" Clark asked.

"Old friends? Everyone is just fine. But, Clark, you don't really want to stay here, do you, son?" Martha asked, suddenly concerned.

"What do you mean?" Clark asked. "I just got back. I want to spend time with you and . . . "

"Clark, please," Martha gently lectured. "I'm fine. I was fine when you left. I was fine when you were away. I'm fine now. I love you very much, but you know hanging around with your mom on the farm isn't what you need to be doing."

Clark knew exactly what his mother meant. He needed to be in Metropolis. He needed to be working at the *Daily Planet*. He needed to be Superman.

"Ma, I think I might be done with all that," Clark explained. "I can't continue to put on that uniform and pretend like I can do everything."

"People know you can't do everything, son," Martha consoled. "You do your best. That's what matters."

That evening, Clark couldn't sleep. His mother's words rang in his head and kept him awake. If he was going to look toward his future, perhaps it was time to look at his past. He crept down the stairs and looked for his mother's scrapbook. He picked it up and began reading

it, skipping ahead to the most recent newspaper articles.

"Superman Saves City from Meteor Shower" was the first headline.

"Astronomers Discover Planet Krypton Intact. Signs of Life Found!"

"Superman Disappears"

As Clark continued reading each of the articles, he began to realize that even more had changed in his absence than he had imagined. The world was different. People's outlooks had changed. For so long they had relied on Superman to save them. So when he left, they became angry. Of course they were! They felt as if their best friend had betrayed them. If the world's greatest super hero could barely handle life on Earth anymore, then what chance did regular people have?

"Will Superman Ever Return?"

They missed him at first. Most everyone did. But as time went on, they lost faith that he would ever come back. Even his biggest supporters eventually admitted to themselves that he was gone. They had decided to move on. It was the only thing they could do. But he wasn't prepared for the final article in the collection.

"Why the World Doesn't Need Superman"

The title stung him, until he saw who wrote it. Lois Lane. He was speechless. There weren't any words to describe what he felt. How could someone he had trusted turn on him like this?

"I see you found my scrapbook," Martha said as she entered the room, startling him. "Did you read everything?"

"Yes. The people don't need me anymore," Clark said, closing the book.

"No, I mean did you start at the very beginning?" asked Martha as she shuffled into the kitchen, leaving Clark on the couch.

"I didn't need to," Clark responded, his voice full of sadness.

"Clark, sweetheart, people thought you weren't coming back. They thought you ran away. They were angry and hurt. You can't blame them for feeling that way," Martha said as she turned on the stove. "How about some warm milk?"

"Jor-El said I've got to be there to catch them when they fall," Clark said, thinking back to the conversation with his birth father. "But it seems like they don't want me to do even that."

The tone in Clark's voice was something his mother had never heard. Hurt.

19

"Come here and bring that book. You didn't look at the whole thing. See?" she said as she opened the book to the first page. "Do you see this headline?"

"It's a Bird. It's a Plane. It's Superman!"

"I'll never forget the day I read that story and saw that photo of you in your costume," Martha said, beaming.

"Uniform, Ma," Clark corrected.

"Oh, I'll call it what I want, Clark," Martha said with a laugh. "There are hundreds of pages here filled with your triumphs and achievements. You've made a difference in so many lives. More than you'll ever know. Now, don't go and let yourself feel down just because of one little article."

Martha Kent stared at her son. He'd never seen her looking so serious. She meant business and had had just about enough of Clark's negativity.

"I understand," Clark said. He smiled at his mother, and she smiled back. Clark had made his decision. He was going back to Metropolis.

The next morning, Clark hastily packed his things, but his mother brought him one last item.

"Here," Martha said, handing him his Superman uniform, looking brand-new and neatly folded. "I made a few updates to it, but I think you'll like it."

"Thanks, Ma," he said as he hugged her.

"Now, you've got to get going or you're going to miss your train," Martha chided.

Clark smiled—as if missing a train mattered to someone who could fly! He grabbed his suitcases, kissed his mother on the cheek, and in an instant, he sped out the door to his bright new future in Metropolis.

5
Superman Returns!

It was just as he remembered. The smells. The people. Everything. The sights and sounds were a little overwhelming for him after all this time. As Clark crossed the street, a cab came out of nowhere and almost hit him.

"Yo, watch where you're goin'!" shouted the angry driver.

"Sorry about that. I should have looked both ways before crossing," Clark called out apologetically.

"What? Is this your first time in Metropolis or somethin'?" the cab driver shouted as he shook his head and drove away.

It wasn't his first time, but it certainly did feel like it. His first memory of Metropolis was from a picture book his father gave him when he was a child. *Great American Cities.* On the cover was a city so big and so amazing that he knew one day he would live there. Within the heart of the city stood not only one of the oldest buildings in the country, but also one of the oldest newspapers, the *Daily Planet.*

As he entered the Daily Planet building, his nervousness grew. *Don't mess up, Kent!*

As Clark got off the elevator, he stood in the waiting area and looked around at all of the framed photos and articles that were hanging on the walls. So many memories were created in these offices. This was Clark's second home, where he worked on stories after hours and stayed up all night to make sure they were perfect.

"KENT!!!!" a voice shouted from deep inside the Daily Planet offices.

Clark smiled and headed back to the office of Perry White, the editor in chief. Mr. White had given Clark his first assignment years ago, and no matter what anyone said about his temper, Perry was a good man who cared for his reporters.

"Good to see you, Kent! But where have you been all this time?!?!"

"Good to see you too, Mr. White . . . I, uh . . . well . . . "

Suddenly, another familiar face entered the room. It was photographer Jimmy Olsen, who was fiddling with his trusty camera.

"He's been traveling the world! Didn't you read all the postcards he sent?"

FLASH!

"Olsen, what have I told you about taking pictures in my office?!" Perry White yelled. "It's annoying. And the next time you do it, you're fired. Understand me?"

"Sure, chief, but you said that the last time. Mr. Kent! Good to see you back," Jimmy said as he gave Clark a strong handshake and a pat on the back.

"It's nice to be back, Jimmy," Clark said smiling.

And Clark meant it, now more than ever. More than anything, he realized that this was what he wanted. To be back in the city, working for a great metropolitan newspaper, surrounded by his friends. But there was one person he still hadn't seen.

"Hey, does anybody know where Lois is?" Clark shyly asked.

"Lane? She's out in the field. Covering the launch of the shuttle *Explorer*," Perry said, pointing to the television monitor in his office. "Now listen, Kent. I hope you're not expecting any handouts, because you're not getting any. As a matter of fact, the only reason I'm giving you a shot again is because we just lost a reporter, and I have a job that needs to be filled."

"I do really appreciate it, Mr. White," Clark said. "Might I ask what happened to the person that I'm replacing?"

"He died, Kent," Perry White said dismissively. "And no, I didn't kill him. Any other questions?"

"No, sir," Clark replied.

"Good, now the first thing we need to do is . . . " Perry's voice

trailed off as he rustled through the papers on his desk. Clark glanced at the television monitor, hoping to catch a glimpse of Lois as she boarded the plane that would be taking the shuttle *Explorer* into space.

"Hey, Jimmy, what's the story with the launch?" Clark asked.

"Well, they're going to launch the *Explorer* from that jet," Jimmy explained, pointing to the shuttle on the television screen. "Instead of using rocket packs to put it into orbit, it's going to ride piggyback on the plane. Then, when it's up high enough . . . BLAST . . . it goes right up and into space. And what's cool is that they're allowing all kinds of reporters to go up there on the jet to cover it. Wish I was going . . . "

"Isn't it kind of dangerous to have a regular plane filled with regular people get up that high into the sky?"

"Who knows?" Jimmy said, realizing the danger for the first time. "I'm sure they've got it worked out. Don't worry, Mr. Kent."

"Listen, Kent, I've got a lot of stuff to do. How about you go find me a story and then we'll chat? Or maybe go grab a bite to eat. And take Olsen there with you."

"Sure thing, Mr. White. Let's go, Jimmy," Clark said, clapping Jimmy on the shoulder.

Clark and Jimmy headed out to get some lunch at the Ace O' Clubs, a local hangout. They found a booth, ordered some food, and settled in to watch the *Explorer* launch on one of the restaurant's televisions.

"Everything is ready to go on the deck of the shuttle," the news reporter announced. "The countdown to launch has begun."

"5 . . . 4 . . . 3 . . ."

"This is going to be good," Jimmy said, as Clark anxiously looked on.

The lights in the bar flickered off and on, causing some customers to joke about the age of the building. The *Daily Planet* also experienced the power outage.

"What in blazes is going on? Did somebody forget to pay the electric bill?" Perry asked.

The lights flickered again and finally went out completely, leaving the entire city in darkness.

Back at the launch site, it looked as if the mission were a failure.

"Ground Control to *Explorer*, we're going to have to stop the

mission until we find out what caused these power outages. Sorry about that."

Suddenly the shuttle's engines powered up, melting the tail of the jet!

"Ground Control to *Explorer*, power down! The mission has been stopped; repeat, the mission has been stopped!"

"*Explorer* to Ground Control. We can't power down the engines, and we can't release the jet, sir! We're taking it with us. The blackout must have damaged the controls. We can't do anything to stop it! We're launching!"

As the shuttle launched, the power returned to the city. Back at the Ace O' Clubs, Jimmy realized the terrible danger Lois was in.

"Holy Christmas!" Jimmy shouted in a panic. "The shuttle is launching! It's melting the jet and . . . and . . . Miss Lane is on board! Mr. Kent, we've got to do something! We've got to call Mr. White . . . we've got to . . . Mr. Kent? Where'd you go?"

Clark was gone. It was, at last, time for the man that Metropolis thought was long gone to make his return. This was too big a job for an ordinary man. This was a job for Superman!

6
A Plane to Catch

The people of Metropolis were not strangers to drama. The citizens had witnessed their share of disasters, both great and small. They had dealt with crime sprees, super-villains, and alien invaders. They were used to danger. But that was then, before their hero left them. These days, when faced with trouble, the response was generally panic. What could they do? They were only human after all. Today, however, they were in for a surprise.

A familiar red and blue figure streaked out of the Daily Planet building toward the burning jet. As he got closer, Superman had to be careful to make sure he did the right thing. His plan was to remove the shuttle from the jet and guide the jet back down to the ground below, as gently as possible, while the shuttle safely glided into space. Superman readied himself for action as he quickly came up to the tail end of the shuttle. Suddenly, the shuttle's reserve rockets fired, completely melting the tail end off the jet. The force was so strong it blasted Superman backward.

This is going to be harder than I thought, Superman realized as he rethought his plan. He took a deep breath and flew back toward the shuttle. Very carefully, he was able to wedge himself in between the shuttle and the jet, separating the two vehicles. He grabbed the shuttle and shoved it up into space, where it was able to reach its orbit.

However, the jet and its passengers weren't out of danger. The

tail of the jet had been melted, and the now tail-free jet was spiraling toward the ground at an alarming speed. Superman raced to catch it. He had to get hold of it before it hit the ground, but that was no easy task. *Lois is on that jet*, he thought. When he caught up to it, he grabbed the right wing in an attempt to slow it down, but the pressure was too much for the damaged wing, and it bent and broke off in his hands. As the jet continued to fall, the other wing snapped off, hitting Superman and then shattering into a million little pieces.

Superman realized there was only one way to stop the out-of-control jet. He flew downward, turning around when he was under the nose of the plane. Using every bit of his strength, he pushed the plane upward. But the danger wasn't over yet. The spiraling jet was headed straight for the stadium, where the season's first baseball game was being played!

"Bottom of the eighth and the Monarchs are down by two with the bases loaded. This might be it, folks!" the announcer complained. "What is that? Wait a second, folks . . . something is coming down from the sky . . . folks . . . we may have a little problem here . . ."

The announcer barely got out the words when the crowd noticed the burning plane heading toward them. The fans ran in all directions in a desperate attempt to escape.

Superman used one more giant burst of superstrength and gave the jet another push, finally stopping it directly over home plate. Gently, he placed the plane down on the field and turned to the stunned baseball fans watching him in the stands. There was complete silence. And then the crowd went wild. Superman was back!

The Man of Steel went to the door of the jet and pulled it off its hinges.

"Is everyone all right?" Superman asked the terrified passengers. The passengers nodded yes. They weren't sure what to say to the man who had just saved their lives.

"You should all stay in your seats until medical attention arrives," Superman said.

***

At the *Daily Planet*, Jimmy Olsen and Perry White cheered the return of Metropolis's greatest super hero.

"He's back, Olsen! He's back! Superman is back! When Lois gets here, I want a full story on his return. I want to know where he's been. I want to know why he left. I want to know everything. And if you're lucky, you might get to take the pictures," Perry said as he patted Jimmy on the shoulder. "Now get out of here!"

**

Meanwhile, at the stadium, a familiar voice called out to Superman from the back of the jet.

"Superman? Superman! It's Lois. Lois Lane . . . . "

While he was in space, Lois' face was the one that gave him the most comfort. At last, Superman was able to see her face in front of him once again.

"Lois, how are you?" Superman asked as he searched for the right words to say. But the right words were hard to come by, given the circumstances. "It's been awhile"

"You can say that again," she said, smiling.

It had been so long since these two had seen each other that they felt like strangers, as if meeting for the first time. They both fumbled, trying to find the right things to say and do. But Superman realized that he had to leave. He wanted to talk to Lois alone.

"I have to go. Take care, Lois," he said, and leaped into the sky.

**

Later, at the *Daily Planet*, a loud argument broke out in Perry White's office.

"Lane, are you out of your mind?" Perry White said as he slammed a cup of coffee down on his desk, spilling it. "You can't be serious! Superman comes back to Metropolis after being away for years, and you want to do a story about the blackout?"

"I just think that something is going on, chief. I mean . . . a city-wide blackout? That's pretty unbelievable for a place like Metropolis. A Superman piece is fine, but people need to know that they're safe."

Deep in her heart, Lois knew that wasn't the reason she didn't want

to do an article on Superman. At one time she was very close to the Man of Steel, but then he went away and things changed. She felt more than a little hurt.

"You know, Lois, I'm sorry to interrupt, but do you really think there's a story in the blackout?" Clark asked as he popped his head into the office.

"Clark? Where did you head off to? I waited at the Ace O' Clubs forever for you. You missed all the stuff with the *Explorer*!" Jimmy said as Clark entered Perry's office.

"Well, if it isn't Clark Kent! Long time no see, Smallville. What brings you back to the city?" Lois teased.

"Actually, a few things but . . . I just wondered why you wouldn't want to do Perry's story on Superman. You used to be pretty close to him."

"You're getting a little personal, Clark," Lois said, tensing.

"Oh, I don't mean to, Lois, but you had such a special relationship with him that I just figured . . ."

"Listen, Clark, what happened between me and Superman is in the past," Lois said, trying to walk out the door.

"Not so fast, Lois," said Perry. "You're not getting off that easy. You want to do a blackout piece? Fine. But you're also getting me an exclusive with Superman, and that's final."

Lois frowned and quickly exited the room, only to come back a moment later.

"I don't even know how to get in contact with Superman!" Lois argued. "It's not like he has a phone number you can just call!"

"That never stopped you before, Lois. You're smart. You'll figure something out. And if worst comes to worst, you can just throw yourself off a building. That always seemed to do the trick before," Perry said, grinning. "Now all of you, get out of my office. I have work to do. And take Olsen with you."

Outside of Perry's office, Lois pulled Clark aside to ask him a very important question.

"Listen, Clark, I'm sorry about being so rude, but it's just a little weird. After all this time, Superman is back, and I just don't know how to feel. Is there any chance that you could get word to him? Tell him I'll

be on the roof of the Daily Planet building tonight at eight o'clock."

Clark stared for a moment, wondering if this meant what he desperately wanted it to mean.

"Got it. Tonight at eight o'clock," Clark nodded.

"And please make sure to tell him that this isn't a date!" Lois said, marching back to her desk.

Clark knew things weren't going to be easy. But would they ever be the same again?

7
Lois Lane

"**S**o, here we are . . . "

Lois Lane wasn't used to being speechless, but standing before Superman, after all this time, she couldn't find the words. These two, once so close, were now almost strangers. Lois attempted to talk, but the words didn't come as easily as they once did. She cursed Perry White under her breath for giving her this assignment as she fidgeted with her recorder. Superman just smiled.

"Shall we start?" Lois finally asked, clicking the recorder and beginning the interview. "Superman, you were gone for quite awhile . . . I know it might seem simple, but where exactly were you?"

"Well, it's kind of complicated," Superman began sheepishly. He wanted to tell her everything, how much he missed her, how much he missed Metropolis, but, he too, was speechless.

"Complicated? You're not getting off that easy," she said as she clicked off the recorder. "I want to know where you were all this time. You didn't say goodbye. You just vanished."

Superman remained silent for a few seconds. He hadn't meant to hurt Lois, but he had, and he was sorry.

"Actually, I left Earth in search of Krypton," he attempted to explain. "I was led to believe that it might not have been destroyed, and I needed to know for sure, so I went looking for it."

Lois clicked her recorder back on. "And what did you find?"

"Nothing. Just a big hunk of kryptonite, floating in space."

"Interesting," she said, "And you didn't think for one minute to tell the people around you where you were going?"

"I didn't mean to hurt anyone. This was something I had to—"

"—do on your own? Save the excuses." Lois began to walk away. In her hurry, Lois tripped, sending the recorder crashing to the ground.

"Here, let me help you," Superman said.

"I don't need your help, and I don't want your help . . . and neither do the people of Metropolis!" Lois stood up, defiant as ever.

"Lois, please. This isn't easy for me. I just need some time. Being back here feels good, but I'm still adjusting. I want to make it up to you. I want to make it up to everyone, and I will. Just give me a chance," he said.

Lois stopped and turned around. What she saw before her was the man she once knew. A man who was committed to truth and justice. It just took her a minute to see it.

"I will. I'm sorry about all this. I just . . . it just hurt when you left, that's all."

"I know I hurt you, but please try to understand," he said. "I'm back now, and I'm not going anywhere."

Lois smiled. Superman smiled back.

"I know you wanted to follow the blackout story but . . . " Superman stopped himself. Before he left he wouldn't have been so careless. It wasn't Superman that knew she wanted to write the blackout story. It was Clark Kent.

"Wait, how do you know about that?" Lois asked.

"Oh, uh, Clark told me," Superman said, trying his best to cover.

"Well, I'm still going to investigate. It's just a little fishy that we experienced a blackout like that at the same time as the shuttle launch," she explained. "And no one seems to know how it started. I have a few leads I'm going to follow up, but nothing solid yet."

"Well, let me know if I can do anything to help," Superman offered.

"Sure. One last thing I want to be clear on," she said sternly. "Things aren't the same as they used to be. Things have changed, and I've changed. We can't just go back to what they were and pretend everything is fine."

"Of course," Superman assured her. "No hard feelings?"

"No hard feelings," Lois said, allowing herself to smile.

For a moment, Lois and Superman just stared at each other.

"All right, I'm sure a cat must be stuck in a tree somewhere," Lois giggled nervously.

"Yes, I think I hear it," Superman said with a conspiratorial smile. "It was good seeing you, Lois."

As Lois waved goodbye, Superman took flight into the night sky. Lois wondered if this was the start of a new chapter for the both of them.

ABOVE: Superman's crystal ship crash-lands near the Kent farm in Smallville, Kansas.
LEFT: Martha Kent cradles Superman near the burning wreckage of the Kryptonian ship.

ABOVE: Clark hides the ruins of the crystal spaceship.
BELOW: Clark takes an early morning walk on the Kent farm.

ABOVE: Young Clark discovers he can fly. BELOW: Young Clark
runs at superspeed and jumps over the cornfields.

ABOVE: Jimmy Olsen welcomes Clark back to work at the *Daily Planet* after being away for 5 years. BELOW: Lois and Clark leave the *Daily Planet* at the end of a long day.

Lois interviews Superman about his return to Earth after
many years away.

Superman catches the Daily Planet globe during the earthquake.

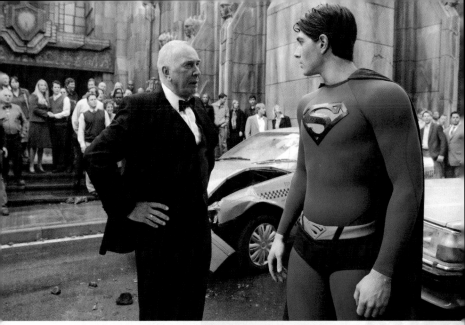

ABOVE: Perry White, editor in chief of the *Daily Planet*, addresses Superman after the earthquake.
RIGHT: Superman checks to make sure everyone is all right.

Superman, the Last Son of Krypton!

8

Soo-per-man!

So what do you think, Mr. Kent? Should I go with the red bow tie or the blue bow tie? I mean, both of them are cool and all, but is the red too much?"

Jimmy squinted at Clark, as if his answer would forever change his life.

"Jimmy, it's just a tie," Clark replied, ignoring him.

"Just a tie?!?!" Jimmy said, staring at Clark like he'd just slapped him. "But this is for my date with Nicole; you know, that blonde intern from Ohio?"

As Jimmy continued to talk, Clark focused elsewhere. His superhearing picked up something in the distance.

"Help! I can't swim! I can't swim!" a boy cried, the sound coming from somewhere near Hob's River.

"Um, wow, Jimmy, those tacos I had for lunch don't seem to be settling with me very well. Will you excuse me for a minute? I just have to go get a drink of water."

Clark was never all that great at covering for his super alter ego, but he'd been away from the game awhile and clearly needed some practice.

"Sure. But about the tie?" Jimmy pleaded.

"Red," Clark said firmly, as he ducked out of the office and into the broom closet.

WHOOSH!

In an instant, a blinding red and blue flash rocketed out of the

building and into the sky, heading toward the Metropolis River.

"I've got you, don't worry!" Superman said, as he scooped the little boy out of Hob's River and set him safely onto the shore.

"This is not the best place to go swimming, son. The undertow around this part of the river is pretty strong. It might be best if you went about a mile down past the bridge, but keep an eye out for changes in the currents. Take care now." And with that, Superman waved goodbye and headed back to the *Daily Planet* to finish his story.

As Superman flew into the sky, he spotted trouble nearby on top of a building as four men robbed a bank. Quietly, two security guards made their way onto the roof in an attempt to stop the robbers. As the four masked men tried to load the stolen money onto a waiting helicopter, things suddenly took a turn for the worse as the robbers pulled out a weapon! One of the security guards fired at the robbers, and in return, the robbers opened fire on the guards. However, they didn't count on Superman swooping in and taking away the robbers' weapons.

"Gentlemen, I would suggest you surrender. It's up to you. We can do it the easy way or the hard way," Superman said, stepping toward the gunman. He stood face-to-face with the quivering criminal. "Feel free to choose the hard way."

The gunman quickly grabbed a small handgun from his ankle holster and aimed directly at Superman. The bullet bounced off Superman's chest as he grabbed the gunman by the collar and hoisted him into the air.

"Not a wise choice," Superman said. Using his superstrength and superspeed, Superman bent the blades of the helicopter around each of the four, wrapping them in a metal body cuff.

The security guards, amazed at what they had just seen, made their way toward their hero.

"Th-thanks, Superman. That was amazing!"

"You're welcome, gentlemen. Now I've got to run. Stay safe," Superman said, and soared into the sky.

This feels good, Superman thought as he rode on an air current. *Out there in space I was so alone. But being back here and helping people, I realize it's really what I was meant to do. I see that now. It's been so*

ng since I've been able to enjoy flying above the clouds. Deadlines are going to have to wait for a moment while I take in the view.

As Superman floated above the city, his X-ray vision spotted something happening in the sewers underneath Metropolis. Two dogs were dangerously close to falling down a drainpipe.

"Well, there goes my break!" he said, diving down through the tunnels underneath the city and approaching the frightened dogs. "I don't know how you two made it down this far, but nothing is going to hurt you," he said, spotting the names on their collars. "Brandy and Charley? All right guys, just stay calm, and I'll get you out of here in no time." Carefully he pulled the dogs into his arms and gently covered them with his cape to protect them as he glided through the tunnel passages and out into the fresh air. The dogs were so excited to be free that they began to squirm around in Superman's arms.

"Easy, you two. We're almost home," he said as one of the dogs wiggled out of his grip and began falling toward the ground. With a quick dive Superman caught him again. "Not so fast there, little guy."

On the ground below, the dog's worried owner spotted Superman and his lost dogs in the sky above. Superman swooped into the man's front yard and handed over the mud-covered dogs.

"Hi there," Superman said. "You might want to get a stronger gate for these two."

"Thank you so much, Superman. I'm Gordon. I'm a big fan of yours! Thank you so much for bringing back our dogs! Martiza, come out here! Superman found the dogs! And bring the girls! You've just got to meet my daughters, Superman. They're big fans."

As the man frantically called for his family, Superman assured him it was all in a day's work.

"Will you stay for dinner, Superman? Grandma is making lasagna," Gordon pleaded.

"I wish I could, but I've got to get back to work," Superman told him.

Gordon motioned Superman closer and whispered in his ear. "I met you a while back, before you left. I was down on my luck. I was going through some tough times. I got into some trouble, you see, and you were the one who helped me. You told me that I was a better person than I realized and that you believed in me. No one had ever told me

that before. I didn't understand it then, but I learned my lesson. Now I have a wonderful family that I love and, well, I just wanted to say than] you, Superman. You changed my life. It's good to see you back." Gordo patted Superman on the back as if they were brothers.

"Gordon, that means a lot. It's good to be back."

Just as Superman was about to leave, he heard a strange cry echo throughout the entire city. It rattled buildings and shook their foundations

"Soo-per-man!!!!!" the cry echoed out.

Sensing that trouble wasn't far behind, Superman took off once more

Looks like I might be in for a busy day, Superman thought. Little did he know what an understatement that was going to prove to be.

9

Project Cadmus

Deep beneath the streets of Metropolis was the headquarters of Project Cadmus, a top secret laboratory that housed some of the most deadly creatures on the planet. Of course the creatures hadn't started out that way. They'd started as simple animals, but through cruel experiments, they had become monsters, who could easily destroy the city. Fifteen minutes before, those beasts had been safely locked away in cages, but now they were on the loose, and Metropolis was soon to become a very dangerous place.

"Code Red in Sector Eight! Repeat: Code Red in Sector Eight! The mutant beasts have escaped the facility!" the intercom blared, sending the warning echoing up and down the corridors.

The scientists who created the mutant animals raced around the facility, trying to figure out how the creatures had managed to escape. The answer became clear when they found one special cell door standing open. Of all the top secret experiments at Project Cadmus, there was one that only three people had knowledge of. This dangerous creature had now escaped. The three scientists stood, staring at the torn metal door, unable to speak as they contemplated the horrible damage that would be done by this beast. This creature was very strong, but his mind was like a small child's. The scientists knew that this creature must have been the one that had set the other creatures free. They also knew that there would be only one person who could possibly bring the creature back.

45

"Soo-per-man!!!"

The repeated cry echoed throughout the city. Arriving on the scene in midtown Metropolis, Superman could barely believe his eyes. The creature that he had to stop looked just like he did, except he was a monster! Dressed in a dark version of Superman's own costume, the bizarre-looking supercreature turned around and greeted the Man of Steel with a big smile, revealing crooked teeth and odd white skin.

"I don't think we've met," Superman said.

The creature stood staring at him, holding a car full of frightened passengers over his head.

"Sooperman! You am finally here! Me want to meet you so much!"

"Please, put that down, and then we can talk. There are people inside. I don't want them to get hurt."

The creature gently put the car on the ground.

"Me am Bizarro! You am Superman! We am brothers! Bizarro needs you help to save city from bad!"

"Listen, friend, I want you to tell me where you came from so we can get you home, okay?"

The Man of Steel tried to communicate as best he could, but Bizarro became very angry.

"You no listen to Bizarro! People in danger!" the distorted twin bellowed.

Suddenly, Bizarro tore out a street lamp and swung it around like a baseball bat, destroying cars and storefronts. Pieces of glass flew everywhere. In the blink of an eye, Superman used his superspeed to get the people out of harm's way. He then sped back to deal with Bizarro.

"Alright, Bizarro, that's enough. We don't want someone getting hurt!" Superman said as he scanned Bizarro with his X-ray vision. What he saw amazed him. The creature was exactly like him, except horribly mutated!

"Bizarro, I need you to listen to me carefully," Superman said firmly. "I need you to tell me where you came from, where your home is."

Bizarro nodded his head and leaped up into the air. As he landed, the ground caved in around him and he fell deep into the sewers

beneath the city. Superman followed, attempting to figure out what on Earth was going on.

"Me show you where Bizarro came from. Follow me!" Bizarro said, marching through the dirty sewer as if he were leading a parade.

A loud roar was heard throughout the sewer system, and Bizzaro's ears perked up.

"Oh, Soo-per-man! You am get to meet Bizarro's enemies!" he said as he ran toward the source of the roar.

As Superman chased Bizarro, he wondered what was ahead in the tunnels. *What in the name of Krypton was that sound? Could there be any more creatures like Bizarro? This is like taking care of a child with superstrength. I've got to find a way to stop this poor creature without hurting him.*

"Look, Soo-per-man!" Bizarro announced after stopping abruptly at a sharp corner in the sewer canal. "These am Bizarro's enemies! You help me destroyed them."

Stepping around the corner, Bizarro introduced Superman to the escaped animal creatures from Project Cadmus. The Man of Steel scanned them with his X-ray vision and was again shocked by what he saw. The creatures—an ape-type creature, a lizard creature, and a hideous gargoyle-like beast, had all been horribly mutated. Whatever they once were, they were no longer anything close. Before Superman or Bizarro could react, the three beasts ran. They were making their way toward the light in an attempt to go above ground.

Capturing these beasts isn't going to be easy, but how do I deal with Bizarro? Superman puzzled. *He won't listen to me and he gets frustrated easily. The only way I'll be able to get him to focus is if he joins me in stopping these creatures.*

"Bizarro, I need your help to stop these creatures, but we're not going to hurt them," Superman explained as if he were speaking to a small child. "Do you understand? We stop them and that's all. Okay?"

Bizarro gave Superman the thumbs-up, and the both of them took off after the escaping creatures.

Meanwhile, on the streets of Metropolis, the ape creature was climbing up a very tall radio tower. Bursting up through a manhole cover, Superman quickly realized he had to stop the creature.

"I'm going after that giant ape. Bizarro, I need you to go find out where the other two have gone. Remember, you're not going to destroy them. Just keep them tied up," Superman said. He hoped his plan to include Bizarro was not a mistake.

"Bizarro use superhearing to find bad enemies!" he said, streaking away.

Flying into the sky, Superman hovered near the giant ape in an attempt to stop him from climbing the delicate tower. But the beast knocked the Man of Steel to the ground. As he got up to confront the beast once again, Superman focused his heat vision upward, turning the tower's metal frame red-hot, causing the creature to lose his grip and fall.

"Don't worry, everyone," Superman said to the gathered crowd, as he flew into the air and caught the falling beast. Suddenly a shot rang out, and the beast went limp and fell to the ground. Superman turned around to see a team of soldiers behind him.

"Excuse us, Superman, but we had to put the beast to sleep to ensure safety," said a young man in a special police uniform who was clearly the leader of a small band of heavily armed and similarly uniformed men. "We can take it from here."

"Pardon me, but who are you?" asked Superman.

"We're the Metropolis Special Crimes Unit," the young man explained.

"Since when did Metropolis need a Special Crimes Unit?" Superman asked further.

"Since you left," the young man snapped. "Now please step aside. We've been assigned to bring these creatures back to Project Cadmus."

"Project Cadmus?" Superman asked. The name sounded familiar, but Superman thought that the Project Cadmus he was familiar with used technology to help humankind, not to run evil experiments. But it did all make sense now. Bizarro. The animal beasts. They were all one big experiment.

"I'm not going to stand by and watch you take these poor creatures back to Cadmus so some lunatic can experiment on them. I'm taking them with me," Superman said.

"I understand you're frustrated, Superman, but please let us do our work," the young man said. "Don't make this harder than it has to be. We have been given orders that we must follow."

"I hope that's not a threat, soldier," Superman said, stepping closer.

Suddenly, one of the soldiers received a call.

"Superman!" a young officer in the back of the group yelled. "We've received word that Bizarro is destroying Metropolis Park."

The field commander and Superman stared at one another.

"Looks like you better get going," the young officer said to Superman. "Timing is everything."

Reluctantly, Superman left the beast in the care of the Special Crimes Unit and sped off to confront Bizarro.

"Bizarro help children!" Bizarro bellowed as he sent a bear flying through the air. "Must keep away bad animals from children!"

As he arrived at the park, Superman quickly realized that including Bizarro in his plans was turning into a disaster. Bizarro was ripping off the animal-shaped seats on the merry-go-round, tossing them into the air, and then hitting them like a baseball.

"Bizarro!" Superman commanded. "Stop it, NOW."

"Bizarro saving children, Superman!" the creature explained like a young child would. "You don't want Bizarro to save children?"

"I want you to stop what you're doing," Superman said, attempting to sound as fatherly as possible.

The childlike Bizarro stopped and turned away, embarrassed.

"Thank you. Now come with me," Superman said, thinking he had gotten through to the childlike monster of a man.

But before Superman realized what was happening, Bizarro grabbed the Man of Steel and held him up in the air.

"Me thought Superman was brother, but you not brother!" Bizarro cried. "You enemy! You try to stop Bizarro from doing good!"

As he struggled to free himself from Bizarro's grip, Superman fired his heat vision at Bizarro's hand, causing him to lose his grip. But Bizarro then used his cold breath to trap Superman in a block of solid ice. Superman easily broke out of the ice and stared at Bizarro.

"This ends, Bizarro. Now," Superman said firmly.

***

Meanwhile, the Metropolis Special Crimes Unit had managed to stop the two other escaped beasts.

49

"This is the Metropolis Special Crimes Unit to Project Cadmus," the young officer radioed. "We've stopped three of your little pets. We're bringing them back to you now, but let me give you a little bit of warning. We're not your personal cleaning service, understand?"

"Yes, yes, of course," came the relieved reply. "What about the fourth creature—the Superman twin?"

The soldier looked into the sky and saw the two flying men fighting.

"Sorry, you're on your own with that one," the young officer said, smiling.

In the sky above, Superman and Bizarro were both getting tired.

"Bizarro, listen to me," Superman pleaded. "I can help you. You and I are alike in many ways. I know you want to help people, but . . ."

"Superman, you am Bizarro's only friend," Bizarro shouted. "Bizarro free animals from Cadmus, because me want to show you Bizarro is hero, too."

"Then come with me. I'll help you," Superman said as he offered his hand to the misunderstood creature. As Bizarro reached out to take Superman's hand, a jolt of electricity fired through Bizarro's body, causing him to pass out. Superman caught him and used his superhearing to check Bizarro's pulse.

He's still alive, but barely, Superman thought. *That electric blast came from out of nowhere. It's almost as if it came from within Bizarro.*

Superman flew down to check on the situation with the animal beasts. The Special Crimes Unit commander was without words as he saw Superman carrying the wounded Bizarro. He cleared his throat and spoke.

"Superman, we were able to stop the rest of the creatures," he reported with a newfound respect. "We're taking them back to Cadmus. I promise you, we'll be watching them."

"I'm taking Bizarro with me," Superman said. The commander nodded as the Man of Steel flew up into the sky, heading straight for his Fortress of Solitude.

10

The Fortress of Solitude

Superman's Fortress of Solitude—hidden in the quiet, white world of the arctic—is a beautiful structure made from ice and crystal. The Fortress was not only his secret hideaway, but a place for him to collect and display his trophies from across the galaxy. The Fortress was also the last remaining piece of Krypton. When Jor-El sent baby Kal-El to Earth, he placed within his ship a crystal that would be able to teach Kal-El all about the Kryptonian civilization. One of the crystals in particular was powerful enough to have created the Fortress of Solitude, so that Kal-El would feel at home. However, to Superman, the Fortress of Solitude was not a home but a place where he could go to be alone and think. Right now he was staring at the containment chamber that housed his mutant twin, Bizarro. He supposed that this would be the closest he would ever come to having a brother.

Look at you, you're so innocent, Superman thought. *You didn't know you were hurting anyone. You were just a pawn in someone's game. But whose? Was it this Project Cadmus, or was it someone or something else entirely?*

"Father! I need to speak to you," Superman called out into the empty chamber. He turned and went to the crystal control bank, gently taking a glowing white crystal and placing it into the main computer. Rays of light lit up the icy Fortress as a hologram of Jor-El activated and appeared in the chamber.

"Hello, my son. You are troubled. Perhaps you are having difficulties understanding Earth cultures?"

"No, Father, that's not it. Today I fought this creature, a twin of myself, except horribly twisted. Someone experimented on him. I felt sorry for the poor creature, but I don't understand why someone would do something like this."

"My son, your questions are good ones. However, you must understand that there are some beings who insist on using science as a way to hurt others instead of to help them."

"I wasn't prepared today. My instincts failed me. I thought I could trust Bizarro because he seemed similar to me, but . . . "

"You tried your best. Perhaps, my son, you . . . you . . . "

All at once the lights went out as Jor-El's skipping voice trailed off and the Fortress went silent.

"Kryptonian Battle Simulation 12," an urgent recorded voice said. "Engage."

As the lights returned, an array of lasers shot out from the crystal computer, straight toward Superman. He dodged left and right, narrowly avoiding them.

"Father, what is this?" Superman asked. He received no answer.

The icy floor of the Fortress began to crumble and break apart, and a giant Kryptonian robot rose up to battle with the Man of Steel. The robot charged at Superman and trapped him underneath its enormous metal body.

Suddenly, the lights flickered again as the robot powered down. Superman pushed the robot off him and back into its icy container.

Something strange is going on here! Superman thought.

It had been a very long time since Superman had visited the Fortress of Solitude, but today he sensed something was very wrong. It was as if someone had been there—and recently.

Superman didn't have much time to think about someone tampering with his Fortress, because his senses just then picked up trouble in Metropolis. Superman flew back to the city he had sworn to protect, hoping he was ready for what he was about to face.

11
You're Fired!

It seemed like just another day in Metropolis. The sun was shining, the trains were running, and Jimmy Olsen was late for work, as usual. As the young photographer slowly crept into the offices of the *Daily Planet*, he was caught by editor in chief Perry White.

"Olsen!" Perry White barked. "What time do I pay you to be here?"

"Nine o'clock sharp, chief!" Jimmy stammered.

"And what time is it now?" Perry bullied.

"It's, um, 9:15," Jimmy said sheepishly.

"That would make you 15 minutes late!" Perry shouted. "You're fired."

Perry stomped into his office and slammed the door as Jimmy stood there, shocked. Suddenly, the Daily Planet building shook. An enormous explosion occurred just outside the building. A crowd of staffers burst into Perry White's office and gathered near the window.

"What are you doing?" Perry turned to look out his window to see what all the fuss was about. "I don't believe it," he said.

Jimmy rushed in to see what it was that had everyone so excited. From what seemed like out of nowhere, a giant volcano had erupted just outside Metropolis, and a flow of lava was headed toward the city. Jimmy quickly grabbed his camera and ran out the door.

"Don't worry, chief! I've got this one covered!" Jimmy yelled excitedly as he rushed for the elevator. "I'm going to get some killer pictures of this thing, so you'll have to rehire me!"

"Olsen, are you insane?" Perry White yelled at Jimmy's back. "Olsen? Olsen!"

Perry's cries went unheard as Jimmy ran to the elevator and then out on the street, ready for action. As Jimmy ran down the street to get a better shot of the erupting volcano, he suddenly found that he wasn't moving as fast as he had been a few seconds earlier.

"Oh, no!" Jimmy said, looking at his new shoes. "The soles of my shoes are melting! Well, it doesn't matter. I've got to get these shots!"

Suddenly, the ground below him made a strange sound, and then lava burst from beneath the street in front of him. But luckily for Jimmy, the Man of Steel scooped him up and dropped him off on top of the Daily Planet building.

"You'll be safe up here, Jimmy," Superman said, smiling.

"But Superman," Jimmy pleaded. "You don't understand. I've got to get some photos of this thing erupting!"

But Superman had something more important for Jimmy to do.

"Jimmy, I need you to go downstairs and get to your computer," Superman explained. "I need you to look up everything you can on earthquakes. See if there are any fault lines in the Metropolis area and map them out. I have a feeling that this is just the beginning of something very bad."

Jimmy waved goodbye to Superman and rushed off to look for the information. Meanwhile, Superman tried to stop the flow of the molten lava. He focused his cold breath on the lava and turned it to solid rock.

Another rumble jolted the city as Superman headed straight toward the giant volcano. Using his X-ray vision, he scanned the surrounding area and looked for anything that might have started the eruption. Superman tried to search his mind for the solution to the problem, but was interrupted by the screams of people in trouble. He turned back toward the city to focus on the cries. He saw that a small girl was caught near another lava flow.

Inside the Daily Planet building, Jimmy searched for any information that might help Superman. An angry Perry White noticed Jimmy and approached him.

"Olsen, what in all of creation did you think you were doing out there?" Perry yelled. "You almost got yourself killed!"

54

"Chief, I just wanted to get some photos of the eruption so you'd rehire me, that's all," Jimmy explained. "But I can't worry about that now. I talked with Superman, and he needs me to find some information about fault lines around Metropolis."

"You're a nutball, Olsen, you know that?" Perry said, shaking his head.

Meanwhile, Superman raced to save the scared little girl, trapped by lava in a dead-end alleyway.

"You're going to be okay, young lady," Superman said in a fatherly voice. "I just need you to close your eyes and count to five, alright?"

The little girl did as she was told while Superman used his breath to freeze the lava flow around her. He gently picked her up and carried her out of harm's way.

"What's your name, little girl?" Superman asked.

"It's Jean," she said, timidly.

"Hold on tightly, Jean," Superman said, smiling warmly. "We're going to find your mommy."

Superman closed his eyes and focused his superhearing. He tuned out the car horns, the people's cries, and the city noise until he could only hear one voice, Jean's mother.

"Jean? Oh, Jean, where are you?"

He focused in on her location and soon placed the frightened little girl safely back in her mother's arms.

"Oh, thank you, Superman," Jean's mother said as she hugged her child tightly. "Thank you so much! You are a miracle!"

Before Superman could respond to the kind words, the ground rumbled yet again as the volcano let off a steady fountain of lava into the air. In an instant, Superman zoomed off to find a way to stop it.

When a volcano erupts, it means that gases as well as molten magma beneath the Earth's crust have built up pressure and need to escape, Superman reminded himself. *There might be a way for me to stop the pressure and change the flow of lava so that it flows deeper underground and out of Metropolis. If I dive into the volcano, I might be able to create vents that could draw the lava away from the city and into Hob's River, where it shouldn't do any harm.*

Before Superman could finish his thought, another blast knocked him backward. Superman recovered and rocketed into the volcano, going deep inside. The unbearable heat and molten magma barely affected his tough skin. He searched in every direction and used his X-ray vision to locate Hob's Bay. Superman tunneled through the volcano, drawing all of the dangerous gas and magma toward the river, where it wouldn't hurt anyone. He burst through the Earth and into the river, where the lava now spilled out, sizzling as it hit the cool liquid. Superman rose out of the river and made sure that the vent he had created changed the flow of lava away from Metropolis. It did, and Superman took off for the Daily Planet building to check on what Jimmy had found out.

12
Volcanic Eruption!

Jimmy knew that the danger had just begun. Since Superman had returned to Metropolis, the city had more than its fair share of dangerous happenings. From an increase in robberies to escaping beasts, it was almost as if Superman's return had brought all this chaos to the city.

"That volcano was just the beginning of some really bad stuff," Jimmy Olsen said, feeling more than a little scared.

"Well, spit it out, Olsen!" Perry yelled as the staff huddled around the young photographer's computer monitor.

"Okay, okay," Jimmy began. "For starters, that volcano wasn't really a volcano. I mean to say it was a volcano today, but it wasn't a volcano yesterday. It was just a mountain until today. Something happened to turn it into a volcano today."

Superman flew into the room and landed behind Jimmy.

"Something? Like what, Jimmy?" Superman asked.

"Superman! Well, that's the weird part. I looked up all the volcanic activity, just like you asked me to do, and I didn't know this, but Metropolis sits on a fault line. It's not a big fault line, but it's a fault line all the same. The only thing that could have caused such an eruption would be an earthquake, so that shaking we felt this afternoon was what caused all this volcanic business."

"But that's not all, is it?" Superman sighed.

"No. All this activity isn't good for that fault line, and, well . . . I'd

say we better get ready for a big one," Jimmy explained worriedly.

"When?" Superman asked.

"Any minute," said Jimmy.

The Daily Planet office erupted into motion.

"What in the world is going on up here?" asked Lois Lane, who had just burst into the room from the stairwell. "I just had to walk up 20 flights of stairs. The elevators are out of order. It took me forever."

"There's going to be an earthquake, Lois," Superman explained. "All right, everyone, I need you all to listen. Slowly make your way down the stairs to the ground. I need you all to stay calm and take care of each other. I'll meet you down there."

As Superman made his way toward the door, Lois stopped him.

"Earthquake? Is that what all those shakes were?" Lois probed. "What did I miss? Wait a second, how do you know there's going to be another one?"

"I just looked it up on the computer," Jimmy smiled.

"What? You're going to listen to Jimmy? Since when did he become an earthquake predictor?" Lois said, ignoring Jimmy and going to her desk. "We're going to be fine."

At that very moment, the Daily Planet building, one of the oldest buildings in Metropolis, began to shake violently.

"Okay, maybe Olsen was right," Lois said, packing up her bag.

"There's no time for that, Lois. You need to move, now!" Superman said, making sure the offices were clear.

Another tremor rocked the city as Superman spotted trouble on the Metropolis Bridge with his super-vision.

"Lois, I have to go," Superman said, "but I need you to get to safety."

"Sure thing, Superman. You too," Lois shouted, as the Man of Steel bolted out the window toward the bridge.

As Superman flew toward the twisting bridge, he felt the Earth moving through the wind currents.

Something's not right, Superman thought. *This is not natural. But there's no time for me to wonder about it now. I've got to get to that bridge.*

The Metropolis suspension bridge shook and twisted as cars and trucks were thrust first into the air and then dropped into the bay. Luckily, most of the passengers were able to leave their cars before they

were thrown into the river, but not all of them. Like a streak of light, Superman used his superspeed to rescue a woman from her car as it plunged into the cold water, leaving her safely on the shore. With no time for talk, Superman flew back and grabbed the broken cables that held the suspension bridge together. Using his heat vision, he welded them together so they wouldn't break, at least for the time being.

Meanwhile, in the city center, buildings were coming apart at the seams as the earthquake rocked Metropolis. Perry, Jimmy, and Lois rushed to find safety.

"So where do we go now?" Jimmy shouted.

"Olsen, can you be quiet for one minute?" Perry roared. "I'm trying to think."

While Perry took a moment to figure out where to go, the famed Daily Planet globe began to tilt back and forth above them. The earthquake had loosened it from its base, and now it was about to roll off the roof and onto the crowds below.

"Chief, should we maybe get inside or underground?" Jimmy suggested.

"What did I say, Olsen? Give me a . . . " Perry yelled, looking up to find the Daily Planet globe hurtling toward him. "Everyone get inside!"

From a mile away, Superman spotted the trouble and raced to the rescue, catching the globe seconds before it hit the ground.

"That was a close one, Superman," said Perry as he came out of hiding and extended his hand to shake Superman's.

"It looks like the worst is over," Superman said, shaking Perry White's hand. "I need to figure out what triggered these natural disasters. I think it might be something worse than we can imagine. I can feel a change in the air. I can't explain it."

Lois ran up to Superman, clutching a radio.

"You're not off duty just yet, Superman," she told him as she held the radio to his ear.

"Riot has escaped from Stryker's Island! If you encounter this deadly super-villain, do not engage him. Stay right where you are. We repeat, Riot has escaped from Stryker's Island!"

Superman sighed. It was going to be a very long day.

13
Riots

Stryker's Island was one of the most heavily guarded maximum-security prisons in the country. Located off the banks of the Hob's River, the chances of a criminal getting in or out of Stryker's Island were slim and none.

"He was a thin man dressed in a skeleton suit! And he had this horrible skull mask on and . . ." explained the elderly woman as she described the frightening man who had stolen her purse to the desk sergeant. Superman used his superhearing and listened to her story as he flew past the Metropolis Police Precinct.

That's Riot, all right, Superman thought. *She described him perfectly. I just don't understand. Even if he escaped from the prison, it would be almost impossible to get off Stryker's Island. But as I have learned too many times, anything is possible with Riot. He can create multiple versions of himself when he's hit very hard—every punch I land creates another duplicate.*

Superman used his X-ray vision to scour the city looking for anything that might lead to Riot. After nothing turned up, he decided to return to the *Daily Planet* to do some research. When he arrived, he was greeted by Lois Lane.

"Clark! Well, you decided to show up after all! Of course, you missed all of the action, but what do you care? You've been traveling the world so long, this must be small news to you," Lois teased.

"Actually, Lois, I was doing some research that I think you might be interested in," Clark said, dropping a large envelope on Lois' desk. "I know you've been looking for information for your blackout story. I talked to a few sources, and I was able to get these charts and maps that outline the power changes in the area the day the lights went out. It pinpoints every location in the city where it could have originated." Clark walked over to his desk, sat down in his chair, and put his feet up.

"Where did you get this? I asked all my connections at the power company, and none of them said they were allowed to give me any information about the power surges."

"Well, Lois," Clark said smiling, "when you're good, you're good."

Little did Lois know that Clark's "sources" included a giant crystal fortress in the Arctic that had one of the most powerful and mysterious computers in the galaxy.

Suddenly, Superman's superhearing picked up a distress call across town. Marlow's Jewelry Store was being robbed!

"I just remembered! I forgot to put money in the meter! I'll be right back, Lois." Clark scurried out the door and into the broom closet. In an instant, he had changed into Superman and flew into the sky, leaving Lois to wonder about his strange behavior.

"But Clark . . . you don't drive," Lois said in confusion.

***

Meanwhile, at Marlow's Jewelry Store, Riot had finally made his long-awaited appearance. The store clerk looked on in fear as Riot, dressed in his skull mask and skeleton suit, tried desperately to open the display case containing the store's most expensive jewels.

"Man, how do you get these things open?" Riot snapped. "Is there a switch or something?"

The frightened clerk shook his head no.

"Oh well, I was going to save this little trick for later, but . . . " Riot threw his arm back and punched the thick glass case in the middle, causing his body to split into two versions of himself!

"Now that I've got a little help, let's see if we can get this done, huh?" Riot said.

"You need a hand, Riot? Please, let me help," Superman suggested as he used his heat vision to superheat the glass, causing Riot to burn his hand.

"Yeowch! Oh, good one, Superman," Riot said, laughing. "You got me there! But you know what happens when you touch me, so don't try any funny business. I'll just be taking these little gifts, and then I'll be on my way."

Superman took a deep breath and released a burst of his cold breath, freezing Riot and his double solid.

"That should hold him," Superman said, addressing the store clerk. "Are you okay?"

Before the man could answer, Superman heard a television news report.

"Hundreds of Riot's duplicates have taken over Metropolis!" the reporter yelled at the camera.

The Man of Steel ran outside and was stunned by what he saw. Hundreds of Riots were running through the streets of Metropolis. Superman sighed and began to round up all of the Riots.

14

S.T.A.R. Labs

"Here's another one, gentlemen," Superman said as he dropped the Riot duplicate into a huge steel holding cell.

"Thanks, Superman," the desk sergeant said. "That makes 455 Riots so far."

For the past 10 hours, Superman had been rounding up the hundreds of Riots, who, were running like madmen through the city, and returning them to a giant holding cell on Stryker's Island.

"This is getting tiresome," Superman said. "I've looked all over Metropolis, but I can't find the real Riot. He's making all of these duplicates to throw me off. But the real Riot is out there somewhere, and if I don't find him soon . . . "

"Take it easy, Superman," the sergeant said, sounding worried. "You look tired. I didn't even know you could be exhausted."

"There's a first time for everything," he said smiling. "Thanks for your help, sergeant. Keep up the good work."

Superman flew into the sky to continue his search. As he soared through the city, an idea occurred to him. He quickly went to the one place in Metropolis that he hoped just might be able to help him.

"Hello, Superman. Welcome to S.T.A.R. Labs," the perky receptionist said. "What can we help you with today?"

"I need to talk to someone in research and development," Superman explained.

Superman was quickly taken to a top secret laboratory. He looked around, staring at all the amazing inventions.

"Superman, I'm Dr. Shah. It's a pleasure to meet you. What can I help you with?"

Superman carefully explained the situation to Dr. Shah as she led him into yet another top secret laboratory.

"Hmmmm. From what you've told me, this Riot character seems unstoppable, but perhaps not," Dr. Shah explained. "We've been working on a special solution that might be able to help you; it turns into a plastic coating that can't be penetrated by flames, cold, or any other extreme conditions. If Riot duplicates when he is struck by something solid, then this might be just the way to contain him. The plastic coating might be able to trap him. Nothing can get in or out. You'd have to surround him with it entirely, but once he's covered, any time he tried to create a duplicate, it would turn his power back on him, and his duplicates would just be reabsorbed into him."

The doctor handed Superman a small ball that felt as if it were made of jelly, and he placed it in a compartment on his belt.

"I can't thank you enough, doctor," Superman smiled as he took off in search of Riot.

All right, I finally have the means to take down Riot, but I still can't find him. Wait a minute! Since Riot's duplicates aren't real people, they wouldn't be hot, like a normal human body, Superman realized happily. *All I have to do is focus my infrared vision and hone in on Riot's body heat, and I'll be able to find the real one!*

Superman searched the city with his infrared vision, searching desperately for Riot's unique energy. Finally he found it in the least likely of places. He dove down to Metropolis Park, where Riot awaited him, sitting proudly on the shoulder of the Superman statue that had been built to honor the Man of Steel.

Found him, Superman thought. *Now to get down there and wrap this up.*

"Predictable, right? But it's so shiny, I just had to!" Riot said, hopping down from his perch. "I just want you to know something, though. I've had a really great time today, but it's just not going to work out between us. We're from different worlds, you and me. You

64

just don't get along with my family!" Riot raised his foot, preparing to stomp on the ground below and create more of his nasty duplicates when Superman delivered his news.

"Wait! Riot, don't! I came here to surrender."

"Right," Riot said as he laughed. "Like I'm going to believe that one."

"Yeah, you're right, I'm a terrible liar. Catch!" Superman said, tossing the ball of jelly from S.T.A.R. Labs at superspeed directly toward Riot, sealing him in an airtight suit. As the skull-faced villain tried to free himself, Superman realized something important that he'd forgotten. He quickly looked around him to try to find what he needed to save the day. He turned to a little girl holding a can of soda. "Excuse me, but may I borrow your straw?" he asked. The girl nodded yes and handed him her straw. Taking a deep breath, he positioned the straw like a dart and tossed it toward Riot, hitting him directly in the mouth. The Man of Steel walked over to him and patted him on the back.

"Sorry about that," Superman said. "I forgot that once the suit sealed up, you wouldn't be able to breathe. Hope this helps. Now, let's get you back to Stryker's."

The Man of Steel turned to wink at the little girl who gave him the straw. and then took off into the sky.

Finally, I've trapped this annoying menace, but I'm not out of hot water yet, Superman realized. *There's still a bunch of duplicates out there that I've got to round up. And then I can go home to some much-needed rest.*

Suddenly, a thought occurred to him. For the past few days he'd been so focused on being Superman that he had forgotten about his life as Clark Kent. He checked the time and realized he was very late for work. Shaking his head, he continued onward to finish finding all the Riot duplicates, wondering if, when it was all over, he'd even have a job to go back to.

15
Parasite

"**K**ent! Wake up!"

It felt like the worst day in the history of being Clark Kent. And Clark Kent had some pretty bad days. In the past week he had had to deal with volcanoes, earthquakes, super-villains, and the worst of all things, newspaper deadlines. Not only was Clark four hours late for work, but today was a major deadline, and his article was nowhere near complete. And worse still, he was sleeping facedown on his desk.

"Sorry, Mr. White, I've just had . . . well, I haven't been feeling very well . . . and . . . "

Clark's voice got softer and softer as Perry White leaned over his desk.

"No more excuses, Kent! You've been making some guest appearances in here lately, but I've not seen you do any actual work. So I'm intrigued as to where your article on that insurance fraud is?"

"See, here's the thing Mr. White . . . "

As Clark tried to come up with an excuse for his missing article, Lois entered the room with an unexpected surprise.

"Clark, you left this on the copier. You should watch where you leave your articles around here. You never know when someone might steal them," Lois said, dropping the article on his desk. Clark's jaw hit the floor as he quickly flipped through the article, reading it at superspeed. It was perfect. Amazed, he handed it to Perry.

"You're real lucky, Kent. Real lucky," Perry said, storming back

into his office and slamming the door behind him.

"Pick your jaw up off the floor, Smallville. It's called a favor," Lois whispered.

"Wow, Lois. I don't know what to say."

"You helped me with my blackout story, so I helped you out with this. We're even," Lois said with a wink. "Actually, you still owe me one. Insurance fraud? Are you kidding me? Why did you ever agree to write about that? I was bored out of my mind."

"Hey, everyone, it's time to go! We're going to be late for the presentation over at S.T.A.R. Labs!" Jimmy yelled, bursting into the newsroom.

Lois and Clark quickly rummaged through their desks and grabbed their recorders. It was not every day that S.T.A.R. Labs made an announcement, but in the craziness of the past few days, the *Daily Planet*'s star reporters had almost forgotten. Along with Jimmy, they jumped into a taxicab and headed to downtown Metropolis for the big announcement.

At S.T.A.R. Labs, the staff hurried to prepare for the big news conference. However, deep within the basement, things were much calmer as janitor Rudy Jones attempted to finish cleaning. Rudy was on a work-release program from prison, and S.T.A.R. Labs had been generous enough to give him a job. He'd been in and out of jail most of his life, but he thought that this time he might turn things around. This might be the job that helped him make his life better.

But something was nagging at Rudy, something he hadn't thought about for a long time. There was a rumor that some of the huge barrels in the basement were used to store money, hidden funds that no one was supposed to know about. The money was safe down there because the barrels were marked as if they were toxic chemicals, and no one would ever touch them. It was a perfect plan. Rudy never really thought it was true, but he had always been curious. For the past month, though, it was as if there were a voice inside him, telling him to open the barrels and see what was inside. It's not that dangerous, the voice would tell him. It's just a little peek. Sure, it was a risk. Sure, it was a gamble, but sometimes in life, you had to roll the dice.

First, Rudy made sure no one had followed him down to the

basement. Then he locked the door. But which one of the barrels was it? He stared at all of the chemical barrels lined up against the wall and wondered. After some careful thinking, Rudy approached one of the toxic barrels.

This is it! I know it is!

Slowly, he unscrewed the top of the barrel and realized a little too late that he had made a horrible life-changing mistake. As he lifted the lid, the heat that came from it burned his hands, so he dropped the lid on the ground. He screamed, but no one could hear him as a swirling green glow of chemicals began to surround him. He tried to crawl to the door to get help, but it was no use. The chemicals had poisoned his body. Rudy knew he was going to die when all of a sudden everything changed. His pain stopped and he was filled with energy. His body was glowing green from the radiation.

It's time to show the world just what Rudy Jones is made of! Rudy thought.

As he made his way toward the stairwell, he noticed a rat in the corner, looking for an exit out of the basement. Without a thought, Rudy fired a bolt of energy at the tiny rat, stealing its life force.

What did I just do? Rudy thought. *What have I become?*

As Rudy made his way up the stairs, he heard the commotion and remembered that today was supposed to be a big day for S.T.A.R. Labs. But instead, today would be the day that everyone in the world learned that Rudy Jones wouldn't be playing the fool anymore.

Up on stage, the big announcement was about to happen. Lois, Clark, and Jimmy looked for seats in the packed auditorium.

"What do you think it's going to be Miss Lane?" Jimmy asked. "A new supercomputer? A flying car?"

"Jimmy, that's the kind of stuff you only see in movies," Lois said, putting a damper on Jimmy's excitement.

"This from a woman who used to date a flying man," Clark said, nudging Jimmy.

"Good one, Mr. Kent!" Jimmy said, laughing.

"Can we please be quiet for a second so I can hear this woman speak?" Lois asked, clearly annoyed. The crowd quieted to hear the big announcement.

The press conference began.

"My name is Dr. Shah, and I'd like to welcome everyone today. All of us at S.T.A.R. Labs have great pride in what we do. It's very important to us that the people of Metropolis support our work. So today, we'd like to give something back. The S.T.A.R. Fund will be a nonprofit foundation that will help . . . "

All at once, the doors exploded open behind the startled Dr. Shah, sending her flying toward the crowd. Superman appeared out of nowhere and caught Dr. Shah just in time.

"That was a close call, doctor," Superman said, leaving the shaken woman on safe ground. "I'll find out what caused it."

As they turned toward the doors, the answer to the question appeared in the burned-out doorway. The creature's body glowed bright green as it extended its hand into the air, showing the crowd just how much energy it had. The beast let out a deafening roar, releasing a pulse of toxic energy! The creature's mouth was filled with sharp teeth. Rudy Jones had become something truly dangerous and was about to make his move.

"Stay back if you don't want to get hurt!" Rudy said. "Now listen up! I am the Parasite and I demand one million dollars delivered to me immediately or . . . or . . . some real bad stuff is gonna happen!"

Rudy was never a good criminal, and he began to wonder if his whole idea was a mistake. Of course, Superman attempted to deal with him by talking things out peacefully.

"Parasite, just calm down," Superman said. "No one needs to get hurt."

"Did you hear me, Blue Boy?" Parasite yelled. "I said I want money, and lots of it!"

Before Superman had a chance to respond, Parasite powered up, his fists crackling with toxic energy.

"Why does it always have to be the hard way?" Superman asked.

As Parasite fired a bolt of energy at him, Superman noticed something strange. Usually his body was able to absorb energy blasts without a problem, but Parasite's energy seemed to be making him weaker. He turned to the crowd and told them to find cover. "Everyone clear the area! I've got this under control."

Parasite ran straight at Superman, biting down on him and sucking the energy from his body.

"Do you feel that, Superman? Do you feel me stealing your energy? People used to look down on me. They used to think I was a nothing. Today all that changes!" Parasite laughed.

"I don't know what's going on, and I don't know what it is you think you have planned, Parasite, but it's not going to happen."

Superman pulled himself out of Parasite's grip and caught his breath. He shook his head and tried to clear his thoughts. Before Parasite knew it, Superman charged at him and knocked him off his feet.

CRASH!

Parasite went flying, blasting through top secret rooms, and landed in the main laboratory, surrounded by top secret inventions. As Superman was about to fly into the building to confront Parasite, Dr. Shah stopped him.

"Superman!" she shouted, running up to the Man of Steel. "Meet me in my laboratory. We need to find out as much as we can about Parasite before it's too late."

Lois approached both of them and made a suggestion of her own.

"Sorry to interrupt, doctor, but I have an idea. Why don't I come to your lab with you, and we can find out what to do about this creature while Superman tries to distract Parasite? Then, once we figure out a way to stop him, Superman can just tune his superhearing to my voice, and I'll coach him."

"Our old superhearing trick, eh, Lois?" Superman said, remembering all the times he had listened for the sound of Lois's voice when he knew she was in danger.

Dr. Shah looked at Superman, who nodded. Then Superman ran to find Parasite.

"Let's go," Lois said, helping the doctor to her lab.

As Superman made his way through S.T.A.R Labs, he grew weaker as he got closer to the dangerous new enemy.

"C'mon, Superman! I'm hungry again!" Parasite taunted as Superman entered the lab.

Parasite ripped a giant metal beam from the ceiling and threw it at Superman, who used his heat vision to cut right through the middle

of it. Superman then grabbed the two pieces and bent them into rings, throwing them back at Parasite and trapping him.

"Do you honestly think this is going to hold me?" Parasite asked.

"Maybe," Superman said, as he flipped a switch on the wall that controlled the super-magnets, causing the two rings to supercharge, jolting Parasite with electricity. But Superman was the one in for a shock—Parasite absorbed the energy charge easily. Breaking free of the rings the now super-energized Parasite fired an energy bolt at Superman, which the Man of Steel quickly dodged.

Parasite then leaped across the room and grabbed Superman by the face. He looked deep into Superman's eyes and sucked the power from his body. However, this time Parasite got more than he bargained for. As the power coursed through Parasite's body, he also absorbed Superman's memories and secrets, specifically, the knowledge that the Man of Steel was really Clark Kent!

"Well, well, well . . . looks like you've got a super-secret, don't you?" Parasite said, laughing. "Who would have thought that the high and mighty Superman was really a puny reporter for the *Daily Planet*?"

Superman forced himself away from Parasite and sent the creature flying.

If Parasite can steal my powers and my memories, Superman thought, *I don't know if I have any hope of stopping it. There's something very odd about him, other than that toxic glow of his, something that tells me he might not know the limit of his own powers yet. And with all that talk from before, something also tells me he's angry about his place in the world. Maybe there's a way to help him? I just hope Lois and the doctor are making some headway.*

Meanwhile, Dr. Shah and Lois attempted to find information on Parasite, using some of the S.T.A.R Labs' technology.

"According to these readings, this creature is a human male," Dr. Shah explained. "Somehow his body has changed. He's able to steal energy from others—he can take their life force. He's also able to absorb enormous amounts of raw energy."

"This isn't looking good for Superman, is it?" Lois asked, already knowing the answer.

"One might be able to assume that the more power he uses, the

faster he burns up the energy that he has taken from other people," Dr. Shah said. "If that holds true we just might be able to stop him by using one of the devices here in my lab."

Dr. Shah quickly scanned the security camera tapes to see if she could identify Parasite's true identity.

"Oh no, it's Rudy!" she said, her head falling into her hands. "He's our janitor. Rudy's on a work-release program from Stryker's Island. He was really starting to turn things around. I don't know why he would do this."

"We'll figure it out, Dr. Shah," Lois said, comforting the doctor.

In another part of the facility, Parasite and Superman continued their battle.

"You think you're so great? You think you're better than me, don't you? Well, you're not needed here anyway, so just go back to wherever you were, and stay there!" Parasite said, firing energy bolts at Superman.

"Listen, I don't know how this happened, but I can help you," Superman said, barely avoiding Parasite's energy.

"You want to help me? I worked my entire life and nobody ever wanted to help Rudy Jones. Nobody! I tried my best all the time and look where it got me," he complained. "I'm not playin' the fool no more! This is my big break, Superman, and I'm gonna take it." Rudy felt more energy coursing through his body. He realized he had all the same powers as Superman! He fired his heat vision as Superman quickly ducked behind a piece of rubble from the damaged lab. As the Man of Steel grew weaker from energy drain, he focused his superhearing and listened for Lois' voice.

"Superman? It's Lois. I really hope you can hear me. There's a way to stop Parasite. His energy powers have a limit. He can overload. Dr. Shah and I are on our way to you now, so you've got to keep him busy until we reach you. Hang in there!"

As Lois and the doctor raced toward the Man of Steel, Parasite attempted to make his final move. He slowly approached Superman, knowing each step he took weakened the Man of Steel further.

"Rudy, don't do this," Superman reasoned with him. "This isn't what you want, is it?"

"How do you know what I want?" Rudy spat angrily. "You grew

up with a good family that loved and took care of you. I saw it when I stole your memories. I saw everything! You had everything you wanted, and you left it all to go find some planet in outer space. You had everything, and you left it! I grew up with nothin', and I still got nothin'!" Parasite yelled.

Superman could feel his body growing weaker. He wondered how much longer it was going to take for Dr. Shah and Lois to arrive. Nevertheless, he still tried to find a way to help Parasite.

"We all go through hard times in our lives," Superman pointed out. "We all question things, believe me, but this isn't the answer. You're draining me, Rudy, and it's killing me. Do you really want that on your conscience?"

"Superman," Rudy said, "I ain't got a conscience."

Without any remorse, Parasite once again used every bit of power he had to drain Superman's energy. At last, Dr. Shah and Lois burst into the damaged laboratory, ready to end the battle once and for all.

"Hey, Ugly, catch!" Lois said as she tossed a small computer chip at Parasite. It attached itself to the energized villain.

As Parasite looked down to see what Lois had done, it was too late. His body started to shake and speed up as he sucked more and more energy from everything around him. Superman looked up at Parasite and hoped this was not the end for Rudy Jones.

"Rudy . . . I'm sorry," Superman said, trying his best to comfort the misguided villain.

Rudy's shaking became more and more violent as a great white flash blinded everyone in the lab. Rudy cried out in pain before his body went limp and fell to the floor. Parasite had used up all of his energy. Now that he had burned out, he'd released his power back into the area, recharging Superman.

"Superman! What a nightmare! That creature almost killed you," Dr. Shah said, checking Rudy's vital signs. "He's still alive, but there's very little brain activity. I knew using that chip would speed his energy intake and cause him to burn out, but . . . " Dr. Shah trailed off. "Superman?"

The Man of Steel stared silently at Rudy's still body.

"Superman, are you all right?" Lois asked.

"No, Lois," Superman said. "I'm not."

Lois went to Superman and embraced him.

"You did everything you could," Lois said, trying to comfort him.

Superman used his cape to cover the smoking body of Rudy Jones. He picked him up gently and walked him out of the building and into the sunlight. He glanced back at the damage and devastation that had been done to S.T.A.R. Labs. The walls were destroyed, important inventions had been broken, and power lines were snapped and sparking. Superman turned and rose into the sky.

16
Time to Stop?

Maybe this was a mistake.

Atop an ice cliff in the Arctic, Superman thought about his recent experiences since his return to Earth. Things hadn't been easy for him.

I thought I could do it. I thought I could return to the life I once had, but it's all just a fantasy. All I want to do is help people, but it never seems to be enough! Superman thought.

Superman let out a loud scream and shoved off from the cliff. He flew into an icy cavern. He pounded its icy walls with his fists as the glaciers around him shook. After a while Superman became tired, and as he took a seat on the cavern floor to rest, he thought about the people of Warworld and wondered if they were okay. He thought about Metropolis and wondered if he wasn't just as big of a threat to the city as Parasite or Bizarro. He thought about his mother, whom he loved beyond anything. And he thought about the words she said to him before he left her.

"People know you can't do everything, son. But you do your best. That's what matters."

But does it really matter? Does it really matter to do your best if you can't bring about real change? Superman thought.

Then Superman heard another voice in his head.

"I got into some trouble, you see, and you were the one that helped me. You told me that I was a better person than I realized and

that you believed in me. No one had ever told me that before. I didn't understand it then, but I learned my lesson. Now I have a wonderful family that I love and, well, I just wanted to say thank you, Superman. You changed my life. It's good to see you back."

Superman rose from the icy ground and flew into another cavern, gliding through the entrance to his Fortress of Solitude and into the prison chamber to check on Parasite. He stared at Parasite and wondered.

I thought I could help you by reasoning with you, but I couldn't, and in the end it didn't matter. Things are getting worse all around the world. Something much bigger is happening, but I can't figure out what it is. Maybe it's time to stop pretending that I can save the world. Maybe it's time to stop being Superman.

17

Heart of Kryptonite

"**Y**ou seem a little down today, Mr. Kent. Everything okay?" Jimmy asked, sitting on the corner of Clark's desk.

"Yeah, sure, Jimmy. Everything's just fine," Clark said.

This is it. No more Superman. It's time to focus on being Clark Kent for once in my life, Clark thought and began typing.

"What are you working on, Smallville?" Lois asked, walking over to Clark's desk to join Jimmy.

"Just working on a story, Lois. I am a reporter after all," Clark replied, clearly annoyed.

"Easy there, Clark, I was just curious. You might fool Jimmy, but there's something going on with you, so spill it," Lois said. She and Jimmy stared at Clark, waiting for his response.

"I just have a lot on my mind right now, okay?" Clark said, too defensively. "And I want to finish this story. So if you don't mind, I'd like to be left alone for a little while."

"I'm not buying it," Lois said. "C'mon Jimmy, you grab one arm. I'll grab the other. Clark Kent, we're taking you to lunch, and there's nothing you can do about it."

Jimmy and Lois dragged Clark through the office, to the elevator, and onto the street below.

"This isn't a good idea, Lois," Clark said, trying to stop them. "I don't want to talk about anything right now."

"Look, Clark, I'm not kidding around," Lois said, staring Clark dead in the eye. "Do you think you're fooling anyone with that 'I'm fine' stuff? Because you're not. Jimmy and I are your friends, and we're here for you, so you can either tell us what's going on with you, or we can stand here until you do."

Clark realized why he always cared about Lois. No matter what the situation was, she never took no for an answer. She always wanted to know who, what, when, where, and why, and she always got what she wanted.

"You win," Clark said as the three friends headed over to the Ace O' Clubs for a bite to eat. After ordering food and making some small talk, Lois began to question Clark about his behavior.

"So what's going on in that head of yours?" she asked.

If only I could tell her that I've given up being Superman, Clark thought, but instead he said, "It's my work. You know how when you work really hard at something, you spend day and night trying your best and giving everything you can, but no matter what, it's just not good enough. You never really feel like the work that you're doing is making any kind of difference." He paused. "That's how I feel."

Clark finished his statement and turned away from his friends, embarrassed. No matter how close he was to these two people, to admit to what he believed to be failure was a tough thing to do. Lois leaned in and spoke softly to Clark, her words coming from her heart.

"Clark Kent, in all the years that I've known you, there's one thing I always admired about you more than anything else. Clark Kent never gives up. When the chips are down, Clark Kent is the one to say, 'Let's keep going.' When any of us doubt ourselves, Clark Kent is the one to push us forward. You know, it's like with Superman . . . "

Clark's ears perked up as he awaited Lois' next thought.

"Do you think that when Superman came back from being away for so long he doubted himself? Do you think he just said, 'Well, I didn't find what I'm looking for, so I guess it's time to throw in the towel?' No! He worked harder than he ever worked in his life, and the people of Metropolis respect him for it. He's never had anything to prove to me or this city, but his presence alone inspires us. We see how hard this man works, and it makes us work harder. We see how good this man is, and it makes us want to be better. My point is that no matter what's on your

mind, just know that all of us admire the work that you do, and we're glad to have you back."

Jimmy and Clark were stunned at Lois' speech.

"Wow, Miss Lane, that was pretty deep," Jimmy said.

Clark stuttered as he tried to find the words to say, but he didn't get the chance to say them as screams came from outside the Ace O' Clubs.

"Jimmy, get your camera!" Lois said, grabbing Jimmy and pulling him with her out the door.

Outside on the street, chaos had erupted! A woman screamed as her watch was ripped off of her arm and soared high into the sky. A man desperately tried to exit his car as its metal parts were torn off and pulled up into the air by some mysterious force. As Clark joined his friends, he noticed something very strange about what was happening.

"Do you feel that tingle in the air?" he asked, as Jimmy and Lois also realized what was going on.

"Yeah, I do . . . it's magnetized," Lois said.

The buildings around them shook as a giant mechanical stomping sound was heard coming down the street. Before they knew it, a shadow was cast over them as they were confronted by one of the city's most dangerous criminals.

"Hello, kids!" said the giant robotic figure, swooping his enormous hand down and scooping up Lois. "Long time no see, Miss Lane!"

"Metallo!" Jimmy shouted.

Years ago, a story written by Lois Lane was able to put convicted felon, John Corben in jail. He had not been happy about it. When he escaped prison, Lois was first on his list of people to destroy. Thankfully, Superman was there to save her. However, during Corben's battle with Superman, he had been fatally wounded; the only thing that saved him was a heart replacement. For days doctors tried to save him, but all of his transplanted hearts failed, and no one knew what to do. His only hope for survival was to replace parts of his body with mechanical ones, making him into a cyborg. It was an experimental operation, but it needed to happen if Corben was going to survive. He also needed a power source of some kind to allow the parts to work.

Finding something to use for power wasn't easy. Against his better judgment, Superman volunteered a piece of kryptonite to serve as

Corben's body's power source, provided he would be monitored and kept locked away.

As Corben spent his time in prison, he noticed his cyborg body getting stronger and stronger every day. Eventually he was able to break out. Taking the name Metallo, he used his new powers to try to destroy Metropolis. He was soon defeated and taken back to prison by Superman, but Metallo's kryptonite heart had almost been the downfall of the Man of Steel. For years Metallo had been sitting in prison waiting for the perfect time to break free and strike back. Today was that day.

"Mr. Kent! We've got to do something!" Jimmy said.

"Yeah, Mr. Kent, why don't you do something?" Metallo said, using his huge cyborg hand to swat Clark across the street. The blow took him by surprise, and Clark began to feel the effects of Metallo's kryptonite heart.

As the mechanical monster marched down the street, Lois called out to Clark in a last attempt to get help.

"Clark! Get Superman!"

But there is no Superman anymore! Clark yelled inside of his head, but then Lois' words came flooding back to him.

"Clark Kent never gives up," she'd said.

"Jimmy," Clark said, "you need to get someplace safe."

"Where are you going, Mr. Kent?" Jimmy asked.

"I'm going to find Superman," Clark said, heading for a phone booth.

18
Metallo

The giant Metallo lumbered through the city, his broad mechanical shoulders ripping into the buildings as he passed.

"Enjoying the view, Miss Lane?" he asked, the eyes within his metal skull-like head glowing bright green.

"The view is very nice, but the company could be better," Lois said. "Let me ask you something, Corben. Who redid your new body? Last time I checked, you were just a normal guy with some metal parts and a kryptonite heart, not some super-robot."

"I had a lot of time to think about things, thanks to you. While I was in jail I slowly began to learn that I could master all forms of metal as well as electronic devices. I could twist them and turn them and absorb their power. What's the matter? You don't like the way I look?"

"Well, it is an improvement," Lois said as Metallo's grip tightened.

"Joke all you want, but this is the last time you'll be able to do so," he said, crushing her body between his metal fingers.

"All right, Metallo. That's enough," Superman said, swooping down from the sky and knocking the stunned Metallo off his feet. As Metallo dropped to the ground, his grip on Lois loosened, and as she fell to the street below, thankfully, Superman was there to catch her.

"You took your time getting here," she said, smiling.

"Nice seeing you, Supes!" Metallo said, revealing his glowing kryptonite heart. Superman's body began to weaken as he flew out of the

area to find safety. He dropped Lois off atop a nearby office building.

"Stay here," Superman told her. "You'll be safe."

"What are you going to do?" Lois asked. "Metallo is 10 stories high, made of metal, and his heart is made of the one thing that steals your powers."

"Never give up," he said, taking off into the sky.

Back on the ground, Metallo continued to cause trouble. He used his magnetic powers to make his metal body even larger.

"You know what the problem is with this city?" Metallo asked. "No one ever thought big! Metropolis is the city of tomorrow, right? Well, it's about time it started acting like it!"

Metallo's arms were crackling with energy. He reached down to the street, thrusting his fists into the concrete and tapping into the power lines beneath the city. His metal body changed the buildings around him to match his robotic form.

"I can do anything!" Metallo laughed.

"Anything? You seem to have a little problem with staying in jail," Superman said, flying out of nowhere and punching Metallo in his metal jaw. "But that's all going to change today."

"Pretty brave, Superman," Metallo said, once again revealing his kryptonite heart. "How do you like me now?"

Superman was caught off guard. He was sure he had enough power to stop Metallo, but the kryptonite was slowing him down, and after awhile he'd be too weak to fight. Metallo touched a metal building and changed it into a gigantic sword, which he used to strike Superman.

"Let's take a little trip, shall we?" Metallo said, grabbing Superman by his cape. Metallo fired his boot jets, and they soared into the sky.

"You know, I have to say I missed you while you were away," Metallo said, tauntingly. "I didn't have anyone to play with. When I saw that you came back, I thought it seemed like a good time to get reacquainted."

"Where are you taking me?" Superman asked.

"Don't you worry about that," Metallo said, laughing. "I've got a little surprise for you."

Metallo landed just outside of Metropolis at a weapons storage area and carelessly threw Superman onto the ground.

"I wanted to show you my new toys, Superman," Metallo said, looking down on the Man of Steel. "Are you ready?"

Metallo ripped the roof off the storage building, and, using all of his power, began to absorb every last weapon into his metal body. He then ripped the roof off another building and stepped inside.

"Like my new shoes?" he asked as his feet changed into two high-tech military tanks.

On the ground below, Superman struggled to find the strength to stop Metallo. Being this close to Metallo's kryptonite heart had weakened and poisoned his body. If he didn't act fast, he might not make it. There's only one thing in the world that could shield Superman from the deadly kryptonite. Lead. There was only one place he knew that might have enough to stop Metallo.

"What's on yer mind, Superman?" Metallo said, picking up the Man of Steel and dangling him in the air. "I'll tell you what's on mine. I'm going to steal Metropolis!"

Superman fired a shot of heat vision directly into Metallo's eyes, causing him to loosen his grip. Superman used the opportunity to get away and form his next plan.

"Where are you goin', Supes? Oh well, doesn't matter. I'm gonna win anyway!" Metallo shouted as he continued to destroy everything around him.

After regaining some of his strength, Superman flew toward Smallville. He had an idea.

It has never been easy to defeat Metallo, but he's always done something to bring about his own capture. This time, though, it looks to be a different story. Metallo has absorbed so many weapons into his body that he is basically unstoppable. But not quite. If I can make some sort of lead suit, I'll be able to fight Metallo without weakening. I remember years ago, Pa had some lead pieces out in the barn that he never got a chance to use. I've got to get to Smallville as fast as I can to find them and make myself a suit, Superman thought. As he arrived on the Kent farm, Superman startled his mother, who was cleaning out the barn.

"Hi, Ma," he said.

"Oh! Clark, what are you doing here? You scared the pants off me!

And you're dressed as Superman! You have to be careful, son. If the neighbors see you . . . " Martha Kent said, excited to see her son.

"I don't have much time. I need your help. Pa used to have some lead pieces from when he was building one of the barns. I need to find them."

"Well, they should be right over there," Martha said, pointing to a dark corner. Before she knew it, Superman kicked into superspeed and began working. He bent and melted the lead, and within a matter of minutes, he had crafted a lead suit and was ready to find Metallo.

"Good seeing you, Ma," he said, kissing her on the cheek.

"I see you took my advice," Martha Kent said, happily. "Go get 'em, son!"

Superman smiled at his mother, and she smiled back as he took off into the sky.

Meanwhile, in Metropolis, Metallo had returned and was rampaging through the city, tearing into buildings and absorbing their electrical power. People ran scared through the streets as he rolled through the city on the giant tanks that were now his feet. At last he made his way to the Daily Planet building. He scanned the entire place with his infrared vision and located his prey. Flexing his mechanical fingers, he ripped off the wall to Perry White's office. Standing inside were Perry White, Jimmy Olsen, and Lois Lane, all of them frightened.

"Great Caesar's ghost!" Perry said as he dropped into his chair.

"Look, it's all my favorite people in one place! The woman whose article put me in jail, the kid that took the pictures, and the guy that published it all!"

Metallo reached in to crush the three when a lead-suited figure streaked by and grabbed Metallo's hand, stopping him from harming anyone. Now, wearing the suit of solid lead to shield him from the kryptonite, Superman was the unstoppable one. He used his amazing strength to twist Metallo's arm, and his heat vision to weld Metallo's fingers together. Metallo screamed in pain as Superman turned to check on his friends.

"Is everyone all right?" Superman asked.

"We're fine, Superman," Lois said. "I like the new suit."

Superman turned back to Metallo, ready to finish the fight.

"All right, Corben, this ends right now!" he said.

As Superman tried to make his move on Metallo, the villain fired a deadly bolt of kryptonite from his eyes.

Normally that would have hurt me, but with this lead suit, I can't feel a thing. I just hope it holds out longer than Metallo does! Superman thought.

Superman and Metallo pounded each other over and over again, and slowly Superman's lead suit began to crack and tear. The slightest bit of exposure to kryptonite still felt horrible to him, but it didn't stop him from completing his task. He grabbed Metallo, and with all his might, he forced the piece of kryptonite out of Metallo's chest. Using his superspeed he flew the rock up into the atmosphere and hurled it into space. Returning to Earth, he found that without a power source, the metal monster began to shrink back to his normal size. Around him, the city had also changed back as everything Metallo touched returned to normal.

"No matter what you do, Superman . . . I'll find a way to escape again, and I'll terrorize everyone you've ever known!" Metallo said, finally falling to the ground like a toy robot.

"And I'll be here to stop you," Superman said, triumphantly.

Joining him on the street below, Lois, Perry, and Jimmy gathered around the fallen Metallo to thank Superman.

"I don't know how many times I've said it, but thank you, Superman," Perry said, grinning.

As Superman lifted up Metallo and flew him off to his Fortress of Solitude for further study, Lois was left with only one question.

"Does anyone know where Clark went?"

EPILOGUE
Only the Beginning

The sun shone brightly on the city of Metropolis as its citizens went about their daily routines. Of course, their daily routines might include the occasional disaster or two. Regardless, they felt safe. Their superpowered champion had returned, and they were happy.

More important, he was happy as well.

"Gee, Mr. Kent, I've never seen you type so fast!" Jimmy Olsen said as he stood by Clark's desk.

"I've got to finish this story on Metallo and get it to Perry by noon, Jimmy. Deadlines and all . . . " Clark said.

"Hey, Smallville, you finish your story yet?" Lois Lane said, approaching Clark's desk.

"Working on it," he said, trying to complete his work.

"I was able to track the source of the blackout. I think I might be on to something really big, Clark. Really big!" she said, giggling with excitement.

"That's great, Lois," Clark said with a smile.

"So you seem to be in better spirits than you were the other day," Lois said.

"Yeah, I guess I am. Thanks for the words of wisdom. You always know the right thing to say."

"It's a gift," Lois said, with a wink.

Suddenly, Clark's ears filled with a high-pitched whistle. He

SUPERMAN
RETURNS™

THE LAST SON OF KRYPTON

EARTHQUAKE IN METROPOLIS!

COMING HOME

I AM SUPERMAN!

BE A HERO!

glanced around the office and noticed that no one else seemed to be affected.

"Clark, are you okay?" Lois asked.

"Yeah, Lois, I'll be fine. Just a headache. Will you excuse me for a moment?" he said, ducking into a nearby bathroom. He splashed water on his face to calm himself, but it did no good. His ears were still ringing with the awful sound. He shook his head again. The sound suddenly stopped, and a voice called out to him.

"Superman?" the voice said. "Superman, can you hear me?"

Clark looked around to see if someone might have been playing a cruel prank as the voice continued.

"Of course, you can hear me. Let me officially honor your return to our fair Metropolis. It's been so long, and we've missed you so much. Things just weren't the same without seeing you flying around in your little tights. I've been leaving messages for you around the city. I wonder if you've gotten them. The first was that Bizarro creature. And then those natural disasters, which were no real fault of my own, I assure you. Then, of course, there was Parasite and Metallo. It's funny how simple men can be manipulated by money and vengeance, isn't it? Anyway, I just wanted to let you know something, so listen carefully. I'm watching you. You might feel safe now, but soon you'll be begging me for mercy. I will destroy everything you've ever cared about, and then I'll destroy you. With my bare hands. Welcome back, Superman. See you around."

Clark's mouth hung open as the voice disappeared.

I knew it. I knew there was one person who brought about the events I have faced since I returned. There's only one person capable of creating that kind of ultrasonic device, and only one person devious enough to threaten me, Clark realized. *Lex Luthor.*

Panic gripped the Last Son of Krypton as he also realized something else.

This is only the beginning . . .